Just Sayin'

Stories from the Heart

Bruce B. Barker

NEWMAN SPRINGS PUBLISHING
320 Broad Street
Red Bank, NJ 07701

First originally published by Newman Springs Publishing 2021

ISBN 978-1-63692-654-4 (Paperback)
ISBN 978-1-63692-655-1 (Digital)

Printed in the United States of America

To my mom and dad, who always stood by me and loved me. And to the Applewood gang, the greatest bunch of neighborhood kids you'd ever want to grow up with.

An act of kindness takes but a moment
but could last a lifetime.
Just sayin'.

Contents

A Kiss to Build a Dream On

It's funny, as we get older, how certain things can trigger a memory.

You see, Michelle was sitting out back by her flower garden. She lived in a small gray house with green shutters. Surrounded by a white picket fence. It was a beautiful summer morning. Sun so warm on her face and the sky so blue. Her mind sorta wandered as she slowly closed her eyes and just listened. A slow smile came upon her face as she listened to the songbirds singing their song. As a gentle breeze blew through the trees, and the sweet smell of her roses gently filled the air. It was only for a moment, then she opened her eyes.

And reached for her cup of hot tea on the table, her hands now all wrinkled. Guess like the rest of her. For she's now in her midseventies. Sometimes a little frail. But always steady on her feet and sharp as a tack.

She drank her last sip of tea. And looked at her watch and thought, *I'm burning daylight, better get moving*, with a chuckle. You see, that's something her husband used to say to her.

She put her cup in the sink. And stopped at the hall mirror. She had the prettiest white hair in an updo. Being careful as she put on her hat. She smiled as she thought how nice it went with her blue dress with pink flowers. And how Henry always loved her in blue.

Huh, Henry? Oh, I'm sorry, Henry is Michelle's husband. They've been married for going on fifty-two years now. High school sweethearts. Back then, he was a little on the shy side.

Seems every time she tells the story of how they met, her whole face lights up, even blushes a little. You see, she was the prettiest blond-haired blue-eyed girl you ever saw, as Henry would say. And of course, anytime he got close to her, he would turn red and would get all tongue-tied.

That is, till one day, she saw him sitting by himself under this tall maple tree, watching our high school baseball team. She walked over toward him. He thought, *OMG...Michelle's walking over. What am I going to do? Okay, it's just a girl...just talk to her. Oh god, she's getting closer.* Soon his mouth felt like the Sahara Desert as his tongue began to knot up.

Michelle said, "Hi, Henry, can I sit down?"

Now in his mind, he thought, *Sure, Michelle, sit down.* But what came out was some sound as he pointed next to him. She smiled and sat next to him. So she said, "Are you enjoying the game?" He quickly nodded his head yes.

She soon reached into her book bag and pulled out this little white bag. As she opened it, she asked Henry if he wanted a kiss. His face went white as his mouth dropped open. All he could do was stare, like a deer in the headlights of a car.

She started to giggle and said, "No, silly, Hershey's Chocolate KISSES." He let out this big sigh and smiled and said sure. One thing Henry loved was Hershey's KISSES. It was magical; after a while, he wasn't tongue-tied. Neither one remembered who won the game but fell in love.

Well, now Michelle took one more look in the mirror and thought, *I'm burning daylight. I'd better get going, don't want to be late.*

You see, it's almost lunchtime at the nursing home where her beloved Henery is. A few years back, Henery was diagnosed with Alzheimer's. Each day, she has to explain who she is. He has good days and some not-so-good days Where he gets confused.

But she doesn't mind much 'cause she remembers how he was always there for her and always loved her—unconditionally.

It's almost time to go as she pulled out this little white bag out of her coat pocket. He looked at it, not knowing what it was. She put something in his hand. He smiled as he opened it to see what it was and said, "Hershey's KISSES, my favorite."

She smiled and remembered so many years ago that she had talked to Henry's mom and explained to her how she liked Henery.

But that Henery was so shy, and how she could not break the ice with him. His mom just smiled and told her how much he loves Hershey's Chocolate KISSES.

"Well, I better be going," she said as she stood up. She gave him a big hug and a kiss on the cheek. As she said, "I love you, Henery," he said, "Thank you, come again." And for a moment, he touched his cheek and said, "You kissed me...why?"

"I wanted to give you...a kiss to build a dream on to remember me." As her eyes filled with tears, she slowly walked away.

Just sayin'.

Flowers from Heaven

Alarm clock went off, it's 5:00 a.m. John's been awake for about fifteen minutes. Just lying there, thinking he might as well get up. You see, at seventy years old, he's had to get up at that time most of his life. And old habits are hard to break. He changed his clothes and went out to the kitchen. Threw open the curtains over the sink. And a warm gentle breeze blew in. He filled the coffeepot with water, and while it's percolating, he went and made the bed and hung up his clothes. As he finished and made his way out, he stopped in the hallway. Under the hall mirror stood a small half-round table with carved legs and a handmade lace doily on top. And on it was a small vase of flowers. He gently grabbed the wilted flowers and put them in the waste basket. He got his coffee and made some toast as he sat at the kitchen table, reading his morning paper. Soon his paper was just about read and his coffee almost gone.

He thought he better get moving, *I'm burning daylight*. He got up and put his dishes in the sink. Walked to the backdoor and on a shelf sat a pair of clippers. He grabbed them on his way out the backdoor and put them in his back pocket. He stood for a moment at the bottom of the step as he looked up at the sky, his hand cupped over his eyes. For the sun was shining like there was no tomorrow. The sky so blue and not a cloud to be seen. He thought, *The Lord sure does make some beautiful days*. He smiled as he walked out to the backyard. Everything was in full bloom. The sweet smell of the flower garden being gently carried in the wind. The squirrels chasing each other as the birds sang their songs.

He stopped at the flower garden. Reached for the clippers from his back pocket. And as he snipped off only the prettiest flowers, a gentle little smile formed on his face as his mind wanders of days long ago. Soon he had a bouquet of flowers cut and went back into the house, putting the clippers away. The house seemed quiet; as John walked, you could hear the floor creak leading to the hallway. At the end of the hall was a beautiful stained glass window. As the morning sun rose, it shined down through the glass on to the table in hues of red, blues, greens, and such. John placed the flowers in the vase and smiles. He looked up in the mirror, the smile now gone as he remembered his Mary. The very love of his life who has long passed. He took out his handkerchief and wiped the tears away.

You see, John made Mary that table one Christmas. It all started one early Sunday morning. Mary couldn't put on her new hat to wear to church because she was also holding her purse and gloves and had no place to set them. John came walking out in his best suit and said, "Mary, I'll hold your things while you put on your hat." Well, now. Mary put on her hat and was admiring it in the mirror when all of a sudden, she began to laugh as she saw John in the mirror behind her with her purse in one hand and folded white gloves in his other hand in his finest suit. They had a good laugh about it as she kissed him and said I love you. And John, with that twinkle in his eye, said, "To the moon and back, Mary, I love you."

That Christmas, John surprised Mary with the table he made, with a big bow on it, underneath the hall mirror. She loved it! Now she had a place for her purse and gloves as she put on her hat. Soon spring arrived, and she found an old cut crystal vase. She thought it was perfect on the table John made her, and she so loved flowers.

The years passed quickly, and now Mary is only a memory in John's heart. But some things never change. The little table under the hall mirror still holds a vase with flowers from Mary's garden.

Just sayin'.

Everything Got Quiet

I was settling down for the night after supper. Thought I'd read a little, so I picked up some Mark Twain whose insight on life always makes me smile.

So with Jazz the wonder dog lying at my feet—well, actually on her back, paws to the heavens, and snoring like a sailor—I opened my book and started to read. Like old friends, it was nice reading about Tom, Huck, and Becky's latest adventures.

After a bit, I got up and got something to drink in the kitchen, let Jazz out for the night before bed, and decided to walk outside.

Now I don't think there's anything better than a warm summer's night. The sound of crickets, and all around you, lightning bugs flashing on and off in the darkness. Stars so bright and seemed almost close enough to touch. And as I sat there, in my rocker, a gentle breeze blew through the pines. Sending its sweet earthy scent through the air.

The moon was full and bright and just seemed to be hanging out with the stars, like two old friends. I wondered if people make wishes on stars anymore, or maybe I'm just showing my age. Guess if they did, they'd have their pick tonight. Me, I kinda like that one to the far left. Let's see if I remember.

> Star light. Star bright
> First star I see tonight
> I wish I may, I wish I might
> Make this wish I wish tonight

Hmmm, well, I made my wish. Sorry, can't tell you what it was. Otherwise it might not come true.

Well, guess I'd better get back inside. Jazz was yawning, and I do want to see if Tom (Sawyer) ever did get that fence painted for his aunt. But it was nice to take a break and sit a spell on this beautiful summer evening.

I miss those Saturdays as a kid that seemed to last forever. Seems life goes by faster now. Yes, it could be we're getting older. But I think that technology has made it quicker. To talk to someone, to learn about something. I think you get the idea.

It's like riding a horse, I guess. Sometimes you need to give him some rein and let him run. While other times, pull the reins back and slow things up a little.

Maybe sit a spell on the back porch after supper and just talk. Or maybe read a book. The sky's the limit.

Just sayin'.

Looks Like We Might Get Some Rain

A farmer out in his field of corn bends down and picks up a clump of dirt. His hands all tan and leathery as he breaks up that hard dry piece of dirt in his hands. Under his breath, he says to himself, "Sure could use some rain." Grounds' been so dry. Been a heat wave going on for quite a while. Hard on the crops but also on the livestock.

Guess we could all use a little rain.

Now depending on where you live, if your house has a metal roof, well, it might sing you to sleep as the rain hits your metal rooftop. As you lie there in bed, all snuggled under the covers. Your windows half-open as the cool air blows in, as the rain gently comes down. You wake up, look out your window at how lush and green everything is. And how the air is so fresh.

Guess we could all use a little rain.

Now I'm telling you, my wife, Jenny, and I love just sitting on the porch, rocking away as we watch a storm roll in over the horizon. As long as the thunder and lightning doesn't get too bad, we let the kids out on the porch with us. We taught them to count the seconds between the lightning strike and the thunderclap. That the smaller the numbers get, the close the storm's getting. I'd just give Jenny a wink as I'd tell the kids, "Yup…sounds like the angels are bowling again. There's another strike! Their hot tonight."

Guess we could all use a little rain.

Ah, young love, we've all been there. Walking hand in hand under an umbrella in the rain.

We all have done it one time or another. She gives you those big brown eyes, dressed in that cute little blue raincoat with baby ducks (all dressed in lil yellow raincoats and hats). Walking hand in hand to the movie theater. All the while as the gentle rain comes down. As she holds you tight under the umbrella.

Guess we could all use a little rain.

Well, bless my soul, soon the storm pass. And out comes the sun and the prettiest rainbow you've ever seen. Those kids run out that front door, faster than a duck on a June bug. All just slippin' and sliding all over the yard. The water overflowed the ditches of fresh warm rainwater.

As they float sticks and boats and things downriver (so I was told). They are wet and muddy from head to toe, all the while laughing and giggling. We hose them off best we can. Give them all baths and put them to bed. And as they close their eyes to fall asleep, I wonder what new adventures tomorrow will bring.

Guess we could all use a little rain.

Guess if there was a moral to this story, life's too short, and things don't always go our way. Sometimes it's better to just relax on the front porch and watch the rain fall.

'Cause behind every black cloud is the sun, just akin to come out and brighten your day.

Just sayin'.

Pumping Gas

It's a beautiful fall day in my little town of Wellington. Looks like we're to get some Indian summer after all. Soon the trees will be bare, and the north winds will blow, bringing the first snow. But for now, I think I'll enjoy this warm fall day. The squirrels are busy gathering nuts for the winter. Getting their nest ready in the trees. Hoping they'll stand up to the north winds of November. I saw a pair of cardinals today. Made me smile. You see, folklore tells us that when you see cardinals around your house, it's actually loved ones from heaven watching over you.

Today I had errands to run and saw I was low on gas. So I pulled in at the gas station, walked in to pay for my gas. And in front of me was this older lady, my guess, in her mid eighties. Her body a little worn, she didn't walk so well, even her voice quivered as she spoke. But the thing that stuck out the most was her smile. It was bigger than Nebraska on a sunny day. By god, when she smiled her whole face lit up. It was contagious; soon I smiled, and the guy behind me was smiling. I watched her walk out to her car as I paid for my gas. I began to smile a little. I slowly walked up to her, so not to frighten her, and asked if it would be okay to pump her gas for her. Now I'm telling you, she smiled so big and kept thanking me like I gave her a million bucks, even though it didn't take me long to fill the car with gas. But while she waited, she began to tell me of her day and all the errands she has to get done. Oh, and that darn gas cap how, in cold weather, it's so hard to get off. I finished pumping her gas. Put that darn gas cap back on. Walked over to open her door. She sat down on the seat, getting one leg in. She was having trouble getting her other leg in. She must've thought I was going to close the door on her leg. 'Cause she hurriedly, with both arms and a grunt, got the other in.

Now it may be wrong—but it made me chuckle. She waved good-bye, and I filled my car and left.

Now I didn't talk about her for a pat on the back. Those who know me know I'm not that way. Maybe me seeing those two cardinals today, how they made me think of my parents and how I was brought up. Yet I wonder if that little old lady will ever know how she made my day and made me smile, almost as big as Nebraska on a sunny day.

Well, I'm burning daylight and almost out of coffee. But I'll leave you with this final thought: an act of kindness takes only a minute but could last a life time. Just saying.

Five Seconds Flat!

Yup, that's all it takes. It seems more and more as technology improves our lives, the human factor is taken out of the equation.

Let me clarify. When we were young as a country, we put a man on the moon and safely brought him home again. Our planes broke the sound barrier. Men and women strived over the years for new ideas to better our lives and make things easier. When I was young and had questions, I turned to books. Like the encyclopedia or the library, or even the school computer.

Today's kids now know how to use a cell phone or kids' computer before they're in school. Some say they're smarter than us. Hmm, I'm not sure. We come to the same conclusion. Lots of times, we used legal pad and a sharp pencil. We thought on our feet. They rely on technology—yes, it's faster. But the human factor isn't always their imagination. And maybe we were brought up differently.

We all rely on technology. Guess we're all guilty of that in some way or another. Case in point, next time you're out and about on a nice summer's day, park yourself on a park bench and just people-watch. Sadly the majority of people will be on their cell phones. Kids as well as adults. Heads down, walking. Surfing the net or on Facebook. "OMG, Debbie! I broke a nail! What am I going to do?"

In the equation, that is the equation of life. Let's put the human being back on the plus side and technology back as a tool. And not like a drug, like a monkey on your back, always depending on it.

Life is so fragile at times yet so beautiful. Just look around you, at the simple things we take for granted. A child's giggle, a smile on an older person. The sweet smell of lilacs in the summer breeze. So why not try it? Put your phone down and look around you. You might smile and say, "Wow, it's a nice day."

What's that? No, I didn't forget. It only takes less than five seconds flat to say or do something nice for someone.

Maybe by saying, "Good morning, how are you today?" Or to open and hold a door for someone, or to just offer to share a bench. You see, in less than five seconds flat, you can make someone's bad day a good day. Maybe even see them smile a little more. It's the human factor.

Just sayin'.

Our County Fair

Well, now, it's fair time once more in my little town of Wellington. You see, our town holds the Lorain County Fair. Now I may be a little prejudiced, but I think it's the best fair around. Now before you folks in other counties get your feathers in a ruffle, guess we all love our fairs and take pride in them.

But let's get back to our fair here in my town. Well, guess I should start by thanking all the men and women who made our town look so beautiful. All the statues are polished, flowers in town are all blooming in their beautiful colors. Flags are flying. Yes, it sure looks pretty downtown.

Hmm, where should I start? There's a couple of organizations like the four H and the FFA (Future Farmers of America). These organizations teach how to raise not only animals but how to raise crops on a farm. You see, having a farm isn't a nine-to-five job. Guess being a farmer, you're part veterinarian, mechanic, weatherman, and a host of other hats he wears just to keep the farm running 24-7. Like birthing time in case the animals need help delivering.

It's not easy, at first, for the kids getting up before school, taking care of the animals like, say, a cow. They buy a calf to raise, learn how to take care of it. And yes, they do get close to their animals. Just as you and I would with a cat or a dog. Then just before fair week starts, they trailer them to the cow barns at the fair. It's exciting showing them. But knowing at the end of the week, it will be sold to someone for food. Yes, there will be tears as they say goodbye to a friend. But that's part of learning to be a young farmer. So at the fair, you might see a young boy lying on top of a cow. His arms around it, as old friends. Guess that's the heart of a young farmer and his friend.

So when you're walking through the barns, seeing the kids doing the barn chores, say hi to them. Maybe ask them about the animals. They won't bite, and sure they'll smile, telling you about their animals.

OMG! Do you smell that? *Yes, it's fair food!* Okay, forget the diet, or it's not healthy for you. Look over there—funnel cake with powdered sugar, fresh-cut french fries, sausage sandwiches with peppers and onions—oh my!

Yes, my friends, if it's fried, it's here, along with cotton candy, candied apples, and such. Yes, Virginia, it's fair week. All the while, the bands are playing. The roar of the tracker pulls going on in the grandstand.

It's that time of year. Just sit a spell, maybe people-watch as you eat a fresh hamburger and fries on a bench. As you listen to some blue grass at a small stage.

There's plenty of vendors to see as they sell their wares or just walk down to the Ferris wheel, catch a glimpse of the whole fair as it takes you for a ride. It's a beautiful summer night. Stars so bright and seem so close you can almost reach out and touch them, as they just hang out with that big old moon.

Then you hear a big *boom!* Followed by a bright burst of reds and yellows. Yup, you guessed it, it was the start of the fireworks. As people stop what they're doing and look up, all the while going *ooh, aah* as the fireworks explode in the sky, bursting out in their beautiful colors. And at the end of the fireworks, there's always clapping and yelling—yay, great fireworks. It's been a long night, and again I wasn't disappointed. What a great fair.

But wait! Can't go just yet. It's tradition to stop at the Wellington band booster building to get a couple of dozen band donuts. Why two, you ask? One, you're going to eat with friends in the car while you're waiting to get out of the fair. Oh and yes, they're that good.

Well, it seems once more, I'm burning daylight. And wouldn't you know it, I'm just about out of coffee. Maybe I'll see if there's any fair donuts left in the kitchen. Ya'll have a good day.

And remember, it only takes a minute for an act of kindness. Might just make someone's day.

Just sayin'.

I See Old People

Well, not really. You see, I was very fortunate to grow up in the small town of Brunswick, Ohio. Now I may be prejudiced, but if you look a little closer, you'll see Byron Drive where I grew up. It was the best neighborhood. And of course, it had the *best* neighbors you could ever grow up with.

A good friend of mine, Mari, coined the phrase "the Applewood gang." Because the majority of us went to the elementary school at the end of the street, Applewood Elementary.

It wasn't just a neighborhood nor were they just neighbors. But they were good friends who cared about you and your family.

Everybody knew your name, and if they saw you out in the yard, they'd wave. And I don't care what you needed, they'd be right there to help you out. Our parents went back and forth with each other. Sharing a good cup of coffee and maybe some coffee cake, laughing and talking about what happened that day with the kids. Which sometimes wasn't a good thing. Because if you ever did something you weren't supposed to be doing, sooner or later, it made it back to Mom and Dad. And well, you get the idea.

I can't begin to tell you how blessed I was to grow up with such great friends from the neighborhood.

No, we didn't grow up with cell phones or computers. We used our imagination, our know-how, and yes, we chewed lots of Bazooka bubble gum. Yet we survived, became successful, and later raised families of our own.

I wish kids today could experience just some of the fun, the laughter, and the friendships we made in that neighborhood.

We climbed the monkey bars, even hung upside down a time or to two impress a cute girl at recess. We'd play four square, and yes, even red rover. Oh and don't forget kickball.

Saturdays seemed to last forever. We'd camp out, cook hot dogs over an open fire, get up early to go fishing, or build forts in the woods. Made slingshots from a branch of a hickory nut tree along with some rubber bands and a small piece of leather.

Maybe go down to Mooney Park to watch the Little League teams play. All the while eating a hot dog in one hand and cherry snow cone in the other, shouting, "Hey batter, batter, batter… Swing!" Then ride our bike all the way home in the now-hot summer sun. All the while thinking of our next adventure.

We played till dark and sometimes past dark. Catching fireflies or playing hide-go-seek. And we knew when it was time to go home. When Mom put the front porch light on, we'd fall fast asleep, dreaming of tomorrow's next adventure.

This year marks our fortieth high school class reunion. Which makes us fifty-eight years old, give or take. A far cry from so many years ago at age six, in our new school clothes, on our first day of school. Being with my friends and neighbors as we began our first day at Applewood Elementary School.

Seems like in a blink of eye, were all grown up. We made it! We finally graduated high school. At graduation, we laughed, we cried, we hugged. All the while saying, "We'll stay in touch." But with this and that, the new job, and, "Hey, I got married," we didn't mean to, but we got busy with our own lives and lost track of each other. No, it doesn't mean we don't care—we do. It's just that our lives are, ever growing and changing as we get older.

And as years went by, and we started to lose friends we knew so many years ago, we think of them and will always miss them. And as we bow our heads and ask God to be with them and their families. We must say goodbye, until we meet again.

So many good memories rush through my mind. Of the Applewood gang and all our adventures we shared together. I fondly think of the times we shared and smiled.

I am truly blessed to call you my friends, and seems I'm a better person that our lives touched. And no matter where you go or what you're doing, you'll always be in my thoughts and prayers because I love you, guys.

And always, always remember.

We're not getting older—just better-looking.

Just sayin'.

I Am

I am my father's son and always proud of that.

I am told I'm just like my mom. Who had a heart the size of a house and always tried to find the good in people.

I am, so far, truly blessed.

I am only human, and I'm sure I have my faults.

I am a believer that a simple act of kindness can change a person's life.

I am a dreamer. For without dreamers, a slinky would be just a coil of wire.

I am a Christian. Who sometimes isn't perfect. Who sometimes doesn't always make the right decisions. But who always knows that "I am never alone in the darkness. For there will always be light."

I am a person who will help someone in need. But become an island when I need help.

I am a romantic. Who still believes in true love and the kiss.

I am someone who believes that when I'm right, that I'll plant my feet and stand firm. Even if I have to stand alone.

I am so many things and at times so few things.

"I am what I am," said my friend Popeye. For those old enough to remember.

Welcome to my world where I am.

Just sayin'.

Will You Be My Valentine?

Said the shy little boy, in a soft voice, to the little girl in his class. He waited till all the other kids went out to recess. He slowly walked over to her and handed her a card marked "TO: ANNIE," printed on the envelope. Along with a few Hershey's KISSES he had in his pocket

Now inside was a very special Valentine's card. You see, he spent the night before going through all the valentine cards his mom got for him to pass out to the other kids in his class. Slowly a smile came across his face. He found it—the perfect valentine's card for Annie.

It had a bear holding a big red heart with an arrow going through it. And it said, "Be my Valentine" on the heart. On the back, he printed, "To: Annie, from Jimmy."

Annie was a pretty little girl with long blond hair and the prettiest blue eyes you ever saw. But Jimmy was so shy and got tongue-tied whenever he was around her. He thought she will never like him.

That is until Valentine's Day.

Well, now, the next day was finally here. The day Jimmy was going to ask his Annie to be his valentine. He decided to ask her at recess. He saw her from across the room. His little heart was beating a mile a minute. He kept looking at the clock. It seemed it was taking forever for the recess bell.

Then finally, it rang. As the kids went out to play, he yelled to Annie, and she came over to him. He thought, *Wow, she sure is pretty*, as she smiled at him. He was so nervous, he almost forgot why he asked her over. But he swallowed hard and held out his hand and gave Annie her card and some Hershey's KISSES he had in his pocket.

He just stood there, not knowing what to do. She opened the card and smiled as she reached into her bag and pulled out a card for Jimmy. His heart was racing as Annie said, "Will you be my

Valentine, Jimmy?" He didn't know how, but he finally got out *yes*. She leaned over and kissed him on the cheek. He could feel his face getting red, and yet he couldn't stop smiling.

Well, now, seems there's a new big man on the playground as Jimmy walked out, holding hands with his little blond blue-eyed Valentine. All the while eating chocolate KISSES.

Just sayin'.

Jazz the Wonder Dog

Yup, that's my Jazz. Her AKC name is All That Jazz. In case you haven't met her, she's an English black Labrador. About seventy-five pounds who still thinks she's a little puppy.

And when she gets wound up—God help you! She comes running at you like Marmaduke on speed. Her tail starts wagging a mile a minute (been known, as she passes, to blow over little kids) as her body turns into seventy-five pounds of rock-hard muscle. All the while that sloppy tongue is hanging out.

Then *wham*! You're on the ground, still dazed, wondering what happened. You feel this big slurp across your face as she's lying next to you, tail wagging, and a look on her face as if to say, "Let's play."

Okay, part of it's my fault. When she was a puppy, I used to roughhouse with her. And shake my fist at her and slide her across the floor. She'd come running back, play-biting my hand, and again across the floor she would go. Needless to say, now at seventy-five pounds, I don't shake my fist at her too often, at least not until I protect the family jewels. In her mind, she's still a puppy (maybe eight pounds). And she's thinking Daddy wants to play. What Daddy sees is, *OMG, here she comes!*

People laugh that I call her Jazz the wonder dog. Well, she never ceases to amaze me. She has a very kind soul. When I'm sick, she's right by my side—with exception if I sneeze. Then she jumps up and makes some distance and then looks at me like, *What the…did that just come out of you?*

She has a heart as big as a house and, as a therapy dog, shows affection and a gentleness to those that need it. With them big ole eyes can just melt your heart. Like most Labs, she uses her paws to get your attention. Or sit next to you, put her head on top of your knee, wanting some attention. In the evening, while watching TV, she lies at my feet, always with one paw touching my foot. Guess she feels safe touching me while she sleeps. And if I should move my foot in her sleep, her paw feels around till she's touching it once more. I've heard she does that because I'm part of the pack.

Hmm, hope I'm the head of the pack. Otherwise I don't think I'd like the view. Just a thought.

We both, as a team, have trained for search and rescue. There are times she's on that scent like a duck on a June bug, and other times, she sees a leaf blowing by and stops as if to say, "Hey, look, a leaf." But that's why you search in groups where one loses the scent, another picks it up.

Some say I'm hard on her. And I am. But she's well trained; but like a child, she to needs structure.

Now that doesn't mean she's not spoiled. She has her own toy box with about twenty-five stuffed animals and toys, five-foot kiddie pool with numerous rubber ducks in different colors and horse balls. Oh, and let's not forget Jazz's spa, a rolling bathtub.

Yes, she's spoiled. Just like after training, I'd stop at McDonald's, get her an ice cream cone. Like a little kid, the first time she had it all over her face. So the other day, I took her with me to run errands and went in the drive-through. She started acting like a junkie getting a fix. Driving out the drive-through, I reached back to give her the cone. She inhaled it, thought I might have lost a hand, then she burped—such a lady.

Well, now you know a little bit about my Jazz.

She always keeps me wondering just what she'll do next. But in the end, she always makes my day. Yes, that's my Jazz.

Just sayin'.

Best Friends

They say, man's best friend is a dog. So you can only imagine a love like no other between a young boy and his dog. Guess you can say I grew up in small-town USA, in the small town of Brunswick, Ohio. Like most small towns, everyone knew your name and was always glad to see you. Growing up, my oldest brother had gotten a new puppy out of a litter my grandma and grandpa had. He named her Ginger; she was part boxer and, I think, pointer. All reddish brown in color with a longer face of a pointer and a short tail like a boxer. Now I'm not exactly sure how old I was—maybe four to five years old. And even though it was my brother's dog, I had found my new best friend.

I shared my peanut butter and jelly sandwiches and tears with Ginger. She always seemed to know if I fell out of a tree or just didn't feel good. She'd lick my tears and sit by me, putting her little head against my chest, letting me know it would be all right.

Soon we both were growing like a weed. Exploring the woods down at Applewood Elementary School. Playing in the creek, building forts. Just running and playing. And when we got tired, we would just lie on the grass on those warm summer days. Her head on my chest, fast asleep. While I looked up at the blue sky, searching for animal shapes in the clouds. Soon I started first grade; she wasn't sure why I was going somewhere without her. But after a while, every day I'd walk home from school. And she'd be waiting at the drive, that little tail wagging a mile a minute. Letting me know she was glad I was home. We shared many adventures growing up. And even though she couldn't speak, when she looked at me, you could see the love in her eyes.

And when she became older, she contracted cancer and was hurting bad. Dad said we had to put her down. He said he'd call the pound. I said, "No, I'll take care of it." And while we waited, I lay there next to her on a warm summer day on the grass like so many times before.

But now I had to say goodbye to my best friend. She looked at me with those big brown eyes as if to say, "I'm sorry I have to leave you, my friend." She licked my tears one last time and laid her head on my shoulder for just a while longer.

You see, friends come in all shapes and sizes—some even in fur. But the few who touch our hearts will always be with us, tucked away in that special place and live on in our thoughts and smiles.

Just sayin'.

Blue Devils Forever

Big doings this weekend. A causal get together on Friday of all classes that graduated from Brunswick. And my class of 1977 fortieth reunion dinner, Saturday night.

So many friends from school I get to see. Some we kept in contact with over the years. And some we lost contact with. But when our eyes met, it seemed like only yesterday.

Forty years is a long time since high school. As we began our journey in life, newly graduates of high school. Some left for college, others to start a new career. Soon we got married, raised our families of our own. And now our kids are having kids. And so life goes on.

Funny as I went to the gathering, I wasn't sure what to expect. Sure we've gotten older, for some gained a little weight. Maybe a few wrinkles. But overall, just a great good-looking group of old friends. So happy to see one another after so many years.

It was like, in many ways, only yesterday. As I looked around the room, old friends getting reacquainted with one another. Laughing about the good times we shared back in high school.

Funny, as we looked back through the old yearbooks, many memories came back like a floodgate opening at a dam. And as I looked around the room, I closed my eyes for a second, and when I reopened them, for a brief second, I saw my friends as we looked back in school; and I just smiled and thought how lucky we all were to share so many good times with.

From Friday night football games, *go Blue Devils!* Going to the drive-in on Saturday night on a warm summer's night with your best girl or guy. Or cutting school on buzzard day in Hinkley for a picnic and, of course, to drink beer.

We shared many good times together. And formed bonds that will last forever. Or at least till the good Lord calls us home.

We bowed our heads in silence to remember good friends that have gone home over the years. We try to remember them all. But we know some we may never know about. But trust God that they're in a better place. It's hard to lose a good friend. We miss them, loved them, but always know we'll see them again.

I guess it's true we can never go back. But for a few hours, good friends from the class of '77 were blessed to get together. We remembered when, as we laughed about good times we had. We ate, we drank, and danced the night away. And one by one, we said our good nights until the next get together.

As for me, all I can say is, I'm truly blessed to call you my friends. Love you, guys.

Just sayin'.

Little Red Kettles

It's funny, the things that can trigger a memory. You know, that something special that can tug at your heart. Soon a twinkle begins to form in your eyes, and a big ole' sappy grin starts to form. For me, it was the sound of a distant bell.

As I looked up, I could see her ringing her bell in front of the store. And yes, next to her was a little red kettle of the Salvation Army. Now I know this time of year, we're all rushing around, trying to get our shopping done. And because we see them all over, we sometimes forget why they are there on a cold snowy blistery day, just ringing that bell.

One day, a long time ago—wait, I'm not that old, LOL. A few years back, close to Christmas, I was over at my mom and dad's house for a visit. My mom needed some things from the store. I told my dad, "I'll drive, I also have errands to run." Seems we weren't the only ones out running errands. The stores were overflowing with shoppers. And as I got out of my car, in the distance, there was this familiar ringing. Sure enough, there was a guy all bundled up in front of the store, ringing his bell. Next to him was the little red kettle of the Salvation Army.

As we both left the store, we both put something in the kettle and wished him a Merry Christmas. After, we left the third store and dropped more money in the pot and wished him a Merry Christmas too.

In conversation, back in my truck, I jokingly said to my dad, "We got a lot of errands left and those kettles are eating through my wallet."

He didn't hesitate as he looked me in the eye and said, "Kid, we've made a good living in construction, and there's a lot of people going through hard times. We need to give back as well as we received. Now I don't care if it's a dollar or even just some change, but never pass a kettle without stopping and putting something in it." And you know, he's right. And I haven't missed one yet.

Guess you're never too old to learn from your father at any age. So now the tradition is mine to carry on. And now when I hear bell ringer's bell, I think of my father's words and two angels up in heaven. And for a brief moment, I look up and smile as I put the money in the red kettle and wish the bell ringer Merry Christmas.

Merry Christmas, Mom and Dad.

Just sayin'.

There Be Changes in the Air

Soon the dog days of August will soon be a memory as September arrives, bringing its majestic fall colors.

A cool breeze is in the air, yet the sun still warms our face.

For us, each season brings new adventures. Maybe going for a long walk in the park with your best girl or guy. Holding hands as you walk through the woods. The trees seem to be on fire as the leaves turn vibrant reds, yellows, and such. All the while, the leaves that have already fallen crunch under your feet as you walk. We stop for some warm apple cider and sit by an open fire and get warm. The smell of the fire seems to fill the air as it crackles and pops as it burns.

There's nothing better than getting up early on a Saturday to travel down to watch a college football game. Being all bundled up with a cold beer and a hot dog with the works. Ref blows his whistle, the hard hits and groans as the two teams battle to win. The marching band sounding so good as they play for their team to win. And maybe a little "Hang On Sloopy" for the crowd.

Yup, baseball caps, sweatshirt, jeans—oh, and hiking boots. Going to a festival out in the woods. The smell of a wood fire was all around us. Venders all dressed out in colonial clothes from days long past. Selling their wares that are handmade such as pottery, candles, brooms, and even the blacksmith as he pounds out his craft to sell. Roving musicians all dressed up, singing their songs.

Ah, smoked turkey legs cooked over an open fire and some bean soup to warm your belly. Oh, and let's not forget fresh kettle corn cooked over an open fire. All sweet and salty and fun to eat as we walk to the next vendor.

And don't forget, just taking a drive in the country. Getting fresh fruit and vegetables at a roadside stand. Maybe pick a bag of apples at the orchard. Shining one up on your shirt as you head to the car, biting into it. That crunch as its juices run down your chin. And soon, you smile as you remember just how good fresh apples are.

Yes, the list goes on and on. You see, each season holds so many treasures that make us smile, and I bet at times, even belly laugh. You see we're always building memories, and the best ones are when they're shared with good friends or that special someone.

A wise man once told me that, "You don't always have to spend a lot of money to have fun. Some Sunday, go for a drive, pack a picnic basket, and see where maybe that road over there goes." Thanks, *Dad!*

I found many hidden treasures just seeing where a road took me off the beaten path.

I hope that maybe you'll keep the tradition going and see where your road leads you.

Just don't forget the picnic basket and blanket.

Just sayin'.

Make Your Peace with God, Bruce!

Once upon a time, as many stories start out, I used to jump out of planes. Yes, not once but four times. Now let me clarify, I did what they call static line jumps. Which means when I jumped, a rope was hooked to my chute and the other end to the plane. Which means when I jumped from the plane, the rope tightened as I fell from the plane and pulled my chute automatically. The chutes were WWII chutes called T-10s; these chutes were very safe chutes. Which in layman's terms, they opened up when they were supposed to.

Ground school consisted of hanging in a chute harness suspended from an A-frame. It sorta looked like those baby swings. You know, the kind with the crank on the side. The instructor says your up, they hook you up to the A-frame in a chute harness, a foot off the ground.

INSTRUCTOR. Okay, you're out on the wing, you're over the site, *go!* Now what do you do next...fall back arching your back, count from 1,001 to 1,010, look up if your chute's not open...pull your reserve.

Sounds simple enough, you're also taught what to do if the chute doesn't open up all the way or doesn't open up.

We're pumped; we're young, we have no fear. We put our chutes on. Oh and by the way, for those who didn't get it, we jumped single. We weren't dangling like a jolly toy, hooked to the front of an instructor.

Two things you always want to remember: One, always make sure your straps are tight; if they're loose and you jump, the full force of your body weight will slam to a sudden stop for a second when the chute opens. Anything caught up in the straps—well, you get the idea. Anyways it's not cool to get on the ground, crying like a little girl in that high voice. The second, don't be last to get on the plane. Yup, you guessed it. I was the first one out. Now these are stripped-out planes, no music playing, just the roar of the engine and a lot of wind. We're all still pumped, taxiing down the runway—we're up, we're airborne. Now everyone's nervous, *Shit, were really doing this*. Okay, we're at ten thousand feet. The instructor took my line and attached it to the floor next to the pilot. He said, "Sit crab-soccer style, facing backwards." Okay, I'm sitting there next to the pilot—you know 50 percent pumped, 50 percent scared, ready to go.

Now just for you to know, to open the door, they have to tilt the plane a little. And yes, of course, to the right, the door side. So without telling me, the plane started to tilt. And the instructor opened the door, and the plane was now back level. Now in those few seconds of this happening—mind you, I'm only a foot from the door—I had a long talk with God. I wanted my mommy, and my butt became a suction cup to that metal floor. Now when the instructor finally stopped laughing, he apologized and said he should've warned me that's how they open the door. Yeah, right.

INSTRUCTOR, (yelling 'cause of the engine and noise from the wind). Okay, we're over the drop zone… Go out on the wing. One foot on post on plane, one on wing post holding on to frame of the wing—*go, go, go!*

I released, arching my back, falling away from the plane. Okay, here's where all that ground training kicks in. You're in free fall, so to speak (only a few seconds); seconds seems like hours. In those few seconds, you're thinking, there's nothing under your feet, wind is rushing all around you. You're thinking, *Oh shit!* Then the shoot opens, you're floating in the air as the plane goes by in slow motion. For some reason, I forgot about counting to 1,001–1,010 and look up to see if the chute's open, LOL. Just relaxing, enjoying the view. I could just about see forever. Yeah, baby, I'm skydiving!

Well, while we're still on the ground, I noticed the chase truck, who gets you if you land out a ways, had a rowboat on a rack on the truck. Just figured they fish. So I'm up there, in my own little world, enjoying the view, when I noticed there's a large quarry to my right, which is now a lake. And the wind was blowing me that way.

Now a little more information about the T-10 chutes: they are a very safe chute to jump with. But the toggles on each side that help steer you—let's just say you don't always turn on a dime when you pull on them. Another point when your parachuting down, you have no depth perception. Which means if you land on water, you can't get out of your chute until you're in the water. Meaning you could drown. And that will also ruin your day.

So by the grace of God, I was able to steer myself away from the quarry back to the drop zone. When I got to tree-top level, I bent my knees, 1, 2, tucked into a shoulder roll, and I was down. That week, I was pumped, I was on an adrenaline high. Fact: it was even better when I was able to poop again. LOL. Just sayin'.

My Dearest Children

Not a day goes by that you're not thought of by your father and I. Even though your all grown up and on your own. Now with careers and family's of your own to raise. Your always close in our hearts.

Your dad and I reminisce as we look at the pictures on the piano. Some made us laugh as others made us cry a little. Like when Jack got his first puppy "Lil Jazz." How he snuck her up to his bedroom to sleep with him. All cozy as two peas in a pod under the covers. Not knowing that they'll soon to become best friends.

Or when Dad for the first time took off Tammys training wheels off her bike. She went pretty far till she hit that bump and crashed. Skinning her knee pretty good. She ran crying into your dad's arms. He held her as she cried, all a while Dad in a soft voice saying, it's ok. He wiped away her tears and her skinned knee. She looked up at your dad with those pretty little brown eyes and said: Can we try it again. Your dad was so proud of her. As He said: "Sure honey" as he smiled and his eyes welled with tears.

We love you kids more than you'll ever know as we always have and always will.

You blessed us with four beautiful grandchildren. All unique and we see you in each of them as they grow. We laugh when you share your stories of their adventures. And of you being a parent as you discipline them. But just like you they turned out pretty good.

Now your dad and I thought long and hard about this letter to you. We wanted you to know just how proud we are of you. We don't want you to remember us and cry. But remember us in love and laughter.

Love Mom and Dad…

A few years have gone by after this letter was written. My wife passed away in her sleep and went home. We decided that whoever survived would sit the family down and read the letter to the kids.

After the funeral, the kids gathered at the house. Slow but sure, I walked over to the drawer where the family Bible was kept. As I carried it over to the table, I opened it to my wife's favorite verse. There laid the letter that was written so many years ago.

As the family sat around the table, I adjusted my glasses and swallowed hard as I opened the letter and began to read.

My dearest children.

Guess if there's a moral to these few words is never take your loved ones for granted.

Just sayin'.

Circle of Life

It's a funny thing, the "Circle of Life."
When we were kids, Saturday's seemed to last forever.
We ran, jumped creeks, climbed trees so tall you could almost see
Wisconsin. We went on all-day bike rides and even camped out.
We quickly grew, now had jobs and nice cars.
We pushed things past the limits, we had no
fear of God or getting hurt. Going to concerts,
enjoying good friends, the sky was the limit.
And always on the go. We fall in love, we marry, with marriage
came responsibility. You now have a house payment and little ones
on the way. Gone are the fast cars, eating in nice restaurants.
Now you split your time between Chuck E. Cheese and soccer.
Mom and Dad come over, and like all grandparents,
love and spoil their grandkids.
Coffee at the kitchen table with Mom and Dad, conversation turns
from the weather and what you have you been up to, to why little
Johnnie got grounded. Mom grabs Dad's hand under the table
next to her. They both laugh at their son's story. She looks into his
father's eyes, and he understands. You see, sitting across from her is
a grown man, a family man, a God-fearing man. But she remembers
back when he was a young boy and all of the mischief he got into.
It kind of tugged at her heart. Her little boy is all grown-up.
Years go by, kids are now in college. Grandma and
Grandpa are a lot older now, and soon grow tired—
and now watch over them from heaven.
Soon you realize you have come full circle.

From the tiny baby that your mother held with so
much love to now being Grandpa holding your son,
Johnny's, newest boy with so much love.
We reach a certain point in our lives where life
starts to take back more than it gives us.
As much as I sometimes hate that fact, I hope it makes us *all* think.
Enjoy each day to the fullest. Always tell the people you love that
you love them to the moon and back.
Because you never know when it's time to go home, and
you're looking down from heaven—it's the circle of life.
Just sayin'.

Once upon a Time

It was bedtime for the twins. They just turned five years old. All wide-eyed and full of vinegar (well, at least one). Always excited to learn new things on their farm. Like most kids, even after a hard day playing and discovering new things, they hated bedtime. Mom made them take a bath—yuck. But they so loved, after mom tucked them in at night, that she always read them a bedtime story.

Oh, I'm sorry, guess you want to know the little ones' names, huh. The little girl is Annie; she has a big heart like her momma. With pigtails, freckles, and always a smile as big as Texas on her face. Loves wearing her bib overalls with her T-shirt and little pink high tops. Sammy is her brother; typical lil boy, baseball cap, T-shirt and jeans, and Spider-Man tennis shoes. Sweetest lil boy you'll ever see. Freckles and a smile that would just melt your heart. That is, until those little horns pop out. LOL

One day, Annie saw a butterfly on the branch of a bush. It was just beautiful, all black and pink and gold. She just stood there, watching it on the branch, opening and closing its little wings. Just smiling and saying, "So pretty." Ole Sammy came running around the comer and stopped for a minute right behind her—then smiled as he shook the bush, and the butterfly flew away. Annie teared up and said, "Don't go," as the butterfly flew away. Sammy just giggled as he watched it fly away. That's just about the time his sweet sister hauled off and hit him and went crying to her mom. Sam just looked at her and went on his way, not a care in the world.

Sammy was walking along, and he found this big stick that fell from the tree. He picked it up, started poking the ground, hitting the bushes with it. That is, till he came upon one of the farm's geese.

Like a big game hunter in deep dark Africa, he creeped up on that goose until he was right behind it. Slowly, ever so slowly, and then *wack* with the stick right on its backside. Well, I'll tell you, that goose jumped five feet at least, going *honk, honk, honk.* Which in people talk is, "Boy, when I catch you, I'm going to bite your butt." Sammy dropped the stick and just started running as fast as those little legs would go. All the while just giggling. That goose was right on his butt, flapping his wings and trying to bite him.

Yup, all the way to the barn where old Blue was lying. You see, old Blue was the family hound dog. He never did like those geese. Always honking while he tried to sleep. He saw that ole goose trying to bite little Sammy. He got up, barking and chasing that old goose right back to the water. Sammy was just laughing as he watched old Blue chase that goose.

Sammy and Blue finally made it up to the house where his mom and sister were weeding the garden as Mom sang them a song. They loved being sung to, and always, always Mom got a big hug afterward.

Nighttime comes early when you're five years old. All clean after a warm bath to get the day's adventures off. All tucked in their beds, sleepy and warm as Mom begins to read, "Once upon a time." You see, kids need to be kids, to go outside and explore. To sing silly songs. To read bedtime stories to. And to never go to bed without a hug and I love you so.

Just sayin'.

My Neighbor Don

It was a warm summer's day. Like most summer days. People were out, cutting their grass, walking their dogs. The mailman waved good morning as he delivered his mail. I had just bought this house in my little town. I saw a diamond in the rough, so to speak. It looked like it had thirty to forty years of neglect. But with a little love and hard work, she's looking like a lady again. I had just ordered a pizza for lunch that day. For some reason that escapes me, I was working in the front yard. And from behind me, I heard kids yelling and laughing. Beeping their horn at some old man who was just sitting on a chair, his dog at his side, watching the cars go by in his front yard. Even though they were just kids at that age, I knew it had to hurt him some. My pizza came, and I decided to walk over and introduce myself to my new neighbor and his dog. I asked if he'd like to have a piece of pizza. He said, "No, but you're welcome to sit and talk a while.

We talked for about a half-hour, and I finally said, "I'm burning daylight, better get back to work on that house."

He thanked me for stopping by and said, "Stop by anytime."

Oh, I'm sorry, let me introduce you to my new neighbor. His name was Don, 6'2", skinny as a rail, eighty-five years young. And he's had every wrinkle an eighty-five-year-old man collected over those years on him with short bristly white hair. Kinda slow to rise but, for the most part, steady on his feet. A little ornery but with a heart the size of Texas. And when he smiled, all those wrinkles seemed to disappear. He'd get that twinkle in his eyes I've grown to like. And of course, that big old smile.

We shared many conversations over the years. Funny, maybe quirky, things popped up. Like his street address, 310 Main Street.

My union laborer's local was 310. He worked for Fisher Foods in Lorain. In the '60s–early '70s, I as well worked Fisher Foods Fazios in late '70s–early '80s. Like a lot of our fathers, Don also served in WWII. And sadly, he also became a POW. And like most POWs, he had medical issues over the years from it.

As our friendship grew, he started telling me about what he went through in the war. Like many soldiers fighting in a war, it was terrible and sometimes gruesome. Later his son, in his sixties, told me he's never heard these stories. His dad came home from the war, never to talk about it. Just picked up where he left off, working and taking care of his family. He was a Mason over the years. Never knew that much about them except he was high up. But soon his wife (the love of his life) had fallen ill, and all his attention was taking care of her and the Masons were no longer.

Sadly I never met her in person. When he talked about her, you could tell their love was like no other and the type of love that's shared by few. I remember he bought her a beautiful oak curio cabinet that she wanted when she was first sick. He filled it with all her knickknacks, making sure to leave the middle top shelf open. You see, she loved angels, and he surprised her with a beautiful porcelain angel figurine. She just loved it, and when he turned the light on, it seemed to shower the angel with light, almost like from heaven.

Years after her death, he still looks at that angel every day. But instead of seeing just a figurine, he sees another angel that's gone to heaven—the love of his life. His mind weary and body tired, he lay down to sleep one summer's eve. And now he has no more pain or loneliness, for my friend is up in heaven with God and, yes, the love of his life. Just sayin'.

Hammocks, Anyone?

Well, now, good morning, my friends.

Just thought I'd share a little story to brighten your Friday morning. I had this hammock, still in the box in my closet. You know, way in the back. Kinda forgot about it. That is, until a friend of mine was moving and asked if I knew anyone who wanted the stand. It was the kind made for a flat-lying hammock.

So I said I'll take it and proceeded to bring it home. Little sanding, some paint, and it looked brand-new. A nice deep emerald green which went well with my hammock, richly woven of bright reds, oranges, and such.

It's the type of hammock that's a double, and you see at the beach where people lie across it. But also comfortable lying lengthwise. I might add that it's made of cotton material and does stretch. So I knew I'd have to adjust it a few times so I'm not lying on the ground. And as you all know, it's not too easy to swing when your butt's touching the ground. Plus people tend to laugh at you.

Okay so I got it all adjusted. Grabbed hold with both hands, lowered my butt gently down.

So far so good, spread the other side out around my body—oh yeah, this feels so good!

Then everything went black!

I didn't know what happened; then I felt this wet slurping sound going up my face. Felt like my eyeball was being sucked out. At the same time, it felt like the wind got knocked out of me.

Well, you guessed it—turned out it was just Jazz the wonder dog, thinking she got a new toy. As she jumped on my lap, got all nestled up next to me as I began to swing in the afternoon sun. Her head lying on my chest, letting out a yawn every so often.

As I was swinging, I thought, *Man, I can get used to this. You know, gentle breeze, sunglasses on, maybe a little bucket of long necks in ice.* Then it happened!

Jazz passed gas! It just creeps up on you and slaps your senses silly. Even my chewing gum lost all flavor. Oh, it didn't bother her, though, she just casually turned her nose upwind.

I said, "That's it! Get off my hammock and stay off. I don't go in your kiddie pool with your baby ducks. You stay off my hammock."

But as you know, I'm a softie and since gave in. We enjoy a little hammock time together as long as she stays on her side and not try to stretch out too much, snore, and yes, pass gas.

Oh, and for those who believe in karma and that God our Creator has a sense of humor.

As I stated earlier, this hammock is a cotton blend. You need to adjust the chains on it so to keep the height when you lie in it so when you're not lying in it, it's a little taut, and lies straight across the stand.

Well, now guess it was a little tighter than I thought. So I grabbed the front side of the hammock with both hands, lowering my chubby little butt ever so gently down on the hammock.

Next thing I knew, I was airborne. Now I'm not quite sure how long my hang time was. But the next thing I knew, I was on my hands and knees, in front of Jazz on the backside of the hammock. I know this 'cause she was licking my face and was holding a little card up with the number 10 on it.

Now you may laugh, but I'm pretty proud of myself. Man my age doing a perfect backward flip (with airtime) and getting a perfect 10.

Guess if there's a moral to my foolishness is: Life is short. It's okay to laugh at yourself, for you know when it's your friends' time, you'll laugh at them.

Just sayin'.

A Little Green House
Down by the River

In a small little town, down by the river, sat a little green house with a white picket fence and a garden of pink roses. There lived a young couple whose names were Julie and Bryant.

They were high school sweethearts. Bryant was head over heels in love with her and soon asked for Julie's hand. Now I'll tell you, that day, I don't think there was a prettier bride. Her dress, all in white and lace. Her beautiful long brown hair all curled and nestled under her veil. Bryant all dressed up in his tux. And he had a grin as big as Texas as he watched Julie walking down the aisle toward him. Well, I'll tell you, it's been a long time since I've had that much fun at a wedding. Why, I even tried to learn the Texas Two-Step. Now they told me later, I danced like a three-legged chicken that night, as they were still laughing about it the next day. *But* in my defense, alcohol was involved.

Well, they moved into their new house. Julie was the school nurse, and Bryant worked at the local sawmill. Julie loved her flower garden, especially pink roses. After supper, he'd take her by her hand and would go for a walk down by the river.

You see, when they were younger, he carved a heart in the tree with their names in it there. He'd always try to steal a kiss. She'd laugh and say, "Tell me you love me first." And he did. She'd push him back, laughing once more, and said, "Tell the whole world you love me."

He smiled as he shouted, "I love you, Julie."

With that, she jumped in his arms and hugged him and said, "I love you too," as she kissed him.

Years go by, now retired. Walking home from church on a warm spring day, Julie's heart gave out, and she fell right by her rose garden. Bryant called, "No...no...Julie, please, Julie, don't go..." He cried for help. "Somebody, please help!" A neighbor heard his cry and ran over to help.

Soon the ambulance came and took his dear Julie to the hospital. For a day and a night, she lay there in a coma. All the while, Bryant was at her side, holding her hand. Praying to God not to take her. She was his world, and he loved her so much.

Soon night turned to day. Julie woke and reached for his hand. He looked up at her with tears in his eyes and said, "I thought I lost you."

She gently smiled as she looked into his eyes. "I'll always be with you...always."

He told her that he loved her. And in a frail voice, she said, "Say it so the whole world can hear it." He got up and leaned down by her ear and ever so gently whispered, "I love you, Julie," in her ear.

Puzzled, she asked him why he didn't say it so the whole world could hear. His eyes welled with tears, and a gentle smile came upon his face. He said, "I did, you're my whole world."

Her eyes welled with tears, she gently smiled as she squeezed his hand. Slowly her eyes closed, and he knew she had gone to heaven— the love of his life, his whole world.

Years later, a young couple walking down by the river noticed an old tree with a heart carved in it. A heart with "Julie and Bryant 4ever" in it. As she touched it, she smiled. And she swore she smelled roses.

Life is not always fairy tales and happy endings. We reach an age where life takes back more than she gives. Always appreciate and love the people in your lives. And always shout out to the world just how much you love them.

Just sayin'.

Sunny-Side Up If You Please

The next time you start feeling sorry for yourself, that things aren't going your way, I want you to think of an egg.

No, I haven't been out in the sun again without my hat; my brains aren't scrambled.

No, it's not easy being an egg.

Poor little guy only gets laid once, and then only by his mother. Now if that doesn't fry your brain, I don't know what does. No, being an egg isn't always what it's cracked up to be.

No, it's not easy being an egg.

Poor little guy, try as he might, he knows timing is everything. It takes him two minutes to get soft and, of course, four minutes to get hard.

No, it's not easy being an egg.

He has to share a room with eleven other eggs. Mostly kept in the dark and in a cool place. A far cry from being kept warm by his mother. Thinking he was her favorite until his brother dropped down next to him.

No, it's not easy being an egg.

Guess if there was a moral to this story.

Life is not always what it's cracked up to be. Sometimes you feel fried and that you don't know what to do. And you reached your boiling point, and things seem pretty hard. But if you just smile and always stay sunny-side up, life will get better, and you can't beat that.

So think of my little friend and always smile and be thankful. And when asked, always say, "Sunny-side up if you please."

Just sayin'.

You're Never Too Old

Have you ever watched an old couple? Sometimes we forget they were once our age, and sooner than later, we'll be theirs. Sure they might not be too stable at times or see so well anymore. All wrinkly and walk with a cane, but when he looks into her eyes, there's still magic there. He looks at her with that special little smile and twinkle in his eyes. He sees that young girl he fell head over heels in love with so many long years ago. He smiles as he gently holds her hand. And then she turns and looks at him and says in a loud voice, *"What did you say?"*

"Oh, for god's sake, Ethel, turn on your hearing aid!"

Well, sir, she did just that, and he told her again. Her eyes filled with tears as she held him and said, "To the moon and back, I love you too."

To a newborn baby, to your first love, to the little blond blue-eyed girl down the street, or that moment when you fell down and skinned your knee. There was only one person to make it feel all better. It was almost magical. Being held in your mom's arms, cradled against her body, kissing you gently, softly telling you, "It's okay, I'm right here."

Even a boy's best friend, his dog, who stood by him through thick and thin. Who's always protected him from harm, and yes, shared his peanut butter and jelly sandwiches that Mom made just for them, and yes, his tears.

You see, your heart isn't just an organ pumping blood. It's also full of love. That warm fuzzy feeling you got when you first fell in love with your high school sweetheart to coming home after a hard day. Your wife's been cooking, cleaning, chasing kids all day. She's a wreck. You look into her eyes and realize how lucky you are. Okay, actually you think the house looks like a cyclone went through it. She could've gotten out of the bathrobe and at least pulled her hair back into a ponytail! But instead you keep quiet 'cause you're hungry, and you know better.

Guess we're never too old to tell someone I love you.

Whoever it may be, you never know, they just might smile and say it back to you. And for those that we will always love, who have died or moved on, there will always be that special place in our hearts where loved ones go. Their memories keep us warm and full of smiles.

Well, I'm burning daylight, and as always, another cup of coffee sounds good. Just sayin'.

She's Such a Dog

It's funny, I've had dogs my entire life. As a young boy growing up, I shared my tears and peanut butter sandwiches with my dogs. We built forts, fought off Indians and even a pirate or two. Just two friends out exploring and having fun.

You see, she couldn't talk, but her tail wagged a mile a minute as we were having fun. All the while giving kisses and jumping on my lap as we lay there under a summer's sun. No, she didn't tell me, but like a good friend, I knew she loved me too.

Seems all my dogs were special, at least in my eyes. They all had their own personalities. But they shared similar traits. They were all very loving and seemed to have good hearts. Or as some would say, they have good souls. And when those big eyes looked at you, it was as if they were saying, "Hello, my friend, I'm glad you're here."

Like many animals, they know when someone's sick or fragile. They move a little slower around them. Maybe lay their heads on their laps, all the while giving kisses, letting them know they too are loved.

Yet they're always alert, senses so keen. Their eyes always searching and the nose smelling the air. And then it happens—*squeak, squeak*! OMG! Someone's got my squeaky toy!

If you're foolishly sitting on the floor, for god's sake, brace yourself—here she comes, seventy-five pounds of muscle who, I might add, still thinks she's that cute little puppy of her youth. Tails wagging a mile a minute as she comes running around the corner. All the while trying to get her toy from you. Slobber everywhere as you think, *Maybe this wasn't the best idea.* Yet you find yourself all smiles. Just laughing, thinking, *What a great pup.*

Sometimes it's like having a kid. There's a great movie on TV, a bowl of popcorn on your lap. And out of the corner of your eye, you see her staring at you. You try to ignore it. But soon, it's like she's in the movie. One eye, you see a rocket landing on a forbidden planet. Yet in the other is her. just sitting there. not moving, just staring.

Finally you can stand it no more! You turn and ask, "Do you have to go potty…want another ham and cheese on rye…did Timmy fall in the well again? No response, okay, bedtime, go to your kennel."

Yes, who could ever forget the times she lies on her back on her bed, so peaceful, like an angel. Then she starts snoring like a drunken sailor. Aww, you might think that's cute. But she's loud, she's not a puppy anymore. Thank God for the TV remote. Sometimes she scares herself awake from her snoring and goes back to the kennel. And it's like, *Why's the TV so loud.*

I love that they lie at my feet and go to sleep. Jazz has to have her paw touching my foot as she sleeps. And if I move my foot in her sleep, she feels around till she finds it. I know you're thinking, "Aww, that's so precious."

Yeah, that is till she passes gas. It slowly creeps up and slaps you in the face. At times, it's so bad she gets up and walks away. The popcorn I'm eating loses all flavor. *"Jazz…kennel!"*

But she's also good company. And after a hard day, I'm greeted with tails wagging, jumping up and down like a rocking horse. Hmm, not sure if that's love or she really has to pee. LOL.

Yeah, she's such a dog. Full of love and friendship. Guess it's true what they say, man's best friend. And you know what, I wouldn't change her for the world.

Just sayin'.

Hey, Doc, Come Quick

A familiar cry after a loud pounding at his door. Being the only doctor for miles around in a small town, he never knew what to expect at any given hour. Delivering a baby, a farm accident, set a broken leg, and yes, even a part-time vet. But whenever he was asked or needed, no matter what the time, he was there.

On a post close to the little white picket fence in the front yard, surrounded by pink roses his wife planted so many years ago, was a sign or his shingle, as it was called in the day.

"Dr. Bryant Barker. MD."

Guess I should start at the beginning. Old Doc Barker wasn't always old. But many years ago, he was fresh out of med school and newly married to his high school sweetheart, Jenny.

You see, he always knew she'd be his wife. He knew the very first moment he looked into her beautiful brown eyes that she was the one for him. And when she smiled at him, however bad the day was going, he felt better.

Well, being fresh out of med school and newly married, he knew he'd have to find something soon. So he sent out many resumes to different hospitals and doctors. Patiently waiting for the mail to arrive each day, only to be discouraged, one by one, by letters saying, "We're sorry but we have no openings."

That is, until one day, a handwritten letter came from a Dr. K. Moody MD to Dr. Bryant Barker MD. Well, he took the letter and sat on the porch rocker and began to read it. Well, it seems old Doc Moody was looking to retire and wanted to train someone to replace him and take over his practice. "And would you be interested? Our little town is called Walnut Grove. A small farming community nestled in the country. An hour and a half from the next nearest doctor or hospital. Would you like to come down for a visit and talk?"

Well, it seems after supper that night, he got to thinking. He asked Jenny to come out on the porch and to let the supper dishes go for a minute. He's got something to tell her. So as they sat out on the porch swing, he began to tell her about old Doc Moody and Walnut Creek.

She sat for a moment, rocking back and forth on the swing. A smile soon appeared as she said, "I love you and will be happy wherever you decide. And Walnut Creek sounds like a wonderful place to raise a family. Let's go for a visit."

Well, now seemed like Jenny and the doctor's wife just hit it off. While Doc Moody, as he was called, showed him his practice. Needless to say, young doctor and his wife felt like they were home. They soon found a little house to live in. With a big yard and a white picket fence. Plenty of room for Jenny's rose garden. For she just loved pink roses.

And old Doc Moody, well, he let out a sigh of relief knowing his patents, his friends, the townspeople would be taken care of. Now that a young fresh doctor was here to take his place.

But it wasn't always a smooth transition. You see, Dr. Barker was young and full of ideas. He was taught on the latest medical techniques but lacked the human touch or bedside manner to talk to people and not at them.

Where old Doc Moody was an old country doctor who not only mended bones but eased the minds of the patients. They trusted him like an old friend. Something the younger doctor must earn— their respect, their trust. Until then, they would always second-guess him and look to old Doc Moody.

It's a good town filled with hardworking, God-fearing people who are always ready to help a friend in need. They were proud of their town and being a farming community. Sometimes money was tight on the farm with this and that and the crops not doing well. Sometimes both doctors got paid eggs or bushels of fruit or something else. They were proud people who always paid their bills.

Either with money if they had it, but at times, bartered with things they grew. Old Doc Barker would just smile and thank them.

But it wasn't always like that. As old Doc Barker remembers, when he first came here, he delivered a baby, and the next day, he got paid, so to speak. The new father came walking up the sidewalk and inside the waiting room—with a pig, had a rope around him and walked him into the office. Like he was walking a dog.

Said, "here you go, Doc. Me and the missus appreciate you delivering the baby. She's a pretty little thing…got lungs like her mother. Appreciate it, Doc, if you keep that between us.

Well, sir, the man shook his hand and handed him the rope and left. Puzzled, the young doctor looked at the nurse, then the pig, and back at the nurse. "What am I going to do with a pig?"

She just laughed and said, "That's your problem."

Turns out, the young doctor and his wife didn't have much money that year. But they ate pretty good. And slowly but surely, the young doctor realized he's not in the city anymore and had to change his ways. Now the townsfolk let him examine them but always still looked to old Doc Moody to see if he was right.

That is, until one sunny summer day, old Doc Moody had a massive heart attack in front of a full waiting room. Young Doc Barker reacted how he was trained and brought Doc Moody back to life and resting as they got him to the hospital, where he fully recovered and decided it's time to retire. Funny how things can change, and I guess people too. Not long after what happened to old Doc Moody, people would see Dr. Barker in town and would break their neck just to say hi. He just smiled, guess they finally accepted him, just as he has of them. Years passed quickly, old Doc Moody has long passed.

Old Doc Barker is pretty used to it now. The loud knock at the door and the familiar "Hey, Doc, come quick."

He grabs his coat and his bag. Kisses Jenny and tells her, "I'll try not to be too late."

She just smiles and says, "They need you, I'll always be here waiting for you," as he rushes out the door. But then he stops for a moment and gives her a smile and a little wink as he turns and walks out into the darkness

No, life isn't always what we think it should be. But maybe it can be something better with someone who believes in you and loves you.

Just sayin'.

He's Just a Soldier

On this day, we remember the American soldier.

They do not always ask for the job. Yet when called to duty, they stand fast and are ready. Some were in the great war and volunteered. Through the years, some were drafted or again volunteered. Some didn't come home.

They come in all shapes and sizes and different walks of life. They train and train, morning to night. All the while getting leaner and learning to be a well-trained soldier. Always at the ready, never knowing when they'll be called to defend our country and our way of life.

Soldiers are someone's son or daughter, husband or wife. And yes, mommy or daddy. They're just like you and me. Trying to work and raise their families. Their job can take them far from home, in extreme heat, carrying an eighty-pound pack. Or alone in a foxhole, under a strange starry sky. Cold and thinking of his family back home. All the while watching for the enemy.

Today is Memorial Day in my little town of Wellington. The yards are all trimmed, American flags hang on the houses. Soon the parade will begin. Like all parades in the beginning, the honor guard carrying our American flag with soldiers from every branch. Some young, some not so young. Yet you see the pride in their eyes as they march by. Their lines aren't always straight. For some, it's been a while since they served. But heads held high, proud they serve our great country.

The tree-covered sidewalk, lined with young and old, all waiting for the parade to pass. "Here it comes," a little boy says to his mom. As the honor guard passes by, people stand up. Some clap and cheer, some stand at attention. Hand on their heart, tears in their eyes. And when they reach the decorated cemetery, a prayer is said, taps are played. All at attention. Some teary-eyed, remembering brothers who didn't come home and thankful for those who did.

Guess we all love a good parade, huh. Especially seeing our flag flying. But freedom is never cheap. Many soldiers, men and women, have died to protect us. So today, we give thanks and honor those, over the years, who kept our country safe. For those still defending us. And for those who didn't make it home.

Thank you.

Oh, and to the young people who think it's okay to burn our flag as well as step on it, when you fall asleep tonight, in your warm bed in your home, always remember the men and women who fought for your rights as you desecrate our flag to help your cause. And as you sleep, they stand guard over you and say, "Not on my watch will any harm come to you."

Yeah, he's just a soldier.

Just sayin'.

Halloween Night in Wellington

There'll be a full moon this Halloween night. First in a long while, I guess. Spooky ghosts and goblins will fill the air with giggles and shouts of "trick or treat." There's a knock at the door, and to my surprise, I saw a cowboy, Dracula, and a little princess. I grabbed my bowl of candy, giving candy to each one. Lastly to the little princess. She looked down into her bag and said, "Hey, mister, don't you have any candy bars?"

I replied, "No, honey, no candy bars."

She said, "The lady next-door gave us a candy bar."

I said, "Okay, give me my candy back."

She got a hurt look on her face and said, "*No!*" as she closed her bag and walked away.

Now I'm sure a few remember being that age and saying, "Trick or treat, smell my feet, give me something good to eat." You know you did.

I'd like to tell you about a friend, his name was Don. He was a widower in his mid eighties. I saw him a couple days before one Halloween. I had asked what he was doing. Well, sir, he said probably just go to bed early.

I said, "No, you're not, you're coming over for dinner and help me pass out candy."

He finally agreed and walked over early Halloween night.

It was a beautiful fall evening, not too warm but just right for trick or treaters. And shining down was the most beautiful full moon you ever did see, just hanging out with a sky full of stars.

I cooked a chicken dinner so good that Andy Taylor's aunt Bea would say, "Oh my."

As we ate, I had put in a WWII movie. He must've liked the chicken, he cleaned his plate and seemed to like the movie. Soon it was time for the trick or treaters. Don was now with his belly stuffed almost as much as a turkey at Thanksgiving, sipping on his coffee while John Wayne was taking the beachhead. I said, "Come on, Don, time to pass out the candy."

He said, "Go ahead, I'm watching the movie."

I shut the TV off, said, "Come on."

I put him on a rocker on the porch and a big bowl of candy on his lap. He gruffly said, "I don't want to pass out candy, you do it."

I said, "Do it till I get back with coffee for us."

And through the window, what do I see? Don was passing out candy, all smiles, asking the little ones who they were (in a crankshaft sorta way). So I came back out with the coffee and biscotti and Gracie, my black lab. It's nice to hear the kids saying thank you as you give out the candy. And from the sidewalk, parents yell out thank you for doing it.

We passed out candy till trick or treat was over. All the while, Don was smiling, talking about this or that. I put the bowls inside, Don says he's heading home. I walked him over to his house, all while he's reminding me he's eighty-five and knows his way home. I said it's a beautiful night, and I was going for a walk anyway. As we walked, he stopped for a moment and looked up at the moon and stars and back at me and smiled. He said, "Tonight reminds me of the first time I took my kids trick or treating. Walking the street, holding their little hands, watching them running up to the houses. Shouting trick or treat before they even got to the door." His eyes teared up as he once more smiled. "Well, thanks, kid, good night."

I said good night and walked home. Stopping for a moment, looking at that beautiful big moon among all those stars in the sky.

All the while smiling and wondering, just how many memories were made on a night like this.

Just sayin'.

Don't Be in a Hurry

You never know when you'll be humbled and truly blessed. I ran to the store real quick and decided to go to the coin open car wash just to get the snow and salt off my car. There was a white minivan in the stall with Florida plates on it. The older man kept staring at the signs and all the buttons, pulling his wallet in and out of his pocket. And me being impatient, wondering why he's moving like pond water on an icy day.

Finally he asked me, "I'm sorry, but I'm having trouble. I feel stupid but could you help me?"

I said, "Sure, come on." He kept thanking me. I told him it's not a big deal. And the only stupid question is the one that doesn't get asked.

Well, we got him situated. He was shivering. I told him if he didn't mind, I'd wash his car and go sit in the car with the heat on. Well, I got it all done, and he wanted to give me money.

"At least let me pay for your wash."

I said, "Thank you, but no."

You came all the way up here to spend Christmas with your elderly mother. Just do something nice for her. As he left, I wished him a Merry Christmas. He teared up and said, "Merry Christmas to you too, and thank you."

Afterward I thought of my dad and how lucky we are to be raised right. I wonder if that old man realized how much he made my day doing something so simple for him. You see, little things to us are big things to others.

Just sayin'.

I Remember When

As a kid, growing up in my little town. Id lie on a soft grassy hill on a warm summer's day. Just me and my dog, watching as the clouds rolled by. Sun so bright and warm on our little faces. Trying to guess what each cloud looked like. We saw clowns and elephants and, yes, maybe a puppy dog or two as they rolled by.

Come Saturday morning, we'd ride our bikes down to Mooney Park where the Little League teams as well as the older Babe Ruth teams played. Got a hot dog and a Pepsi and watched a baseball game or two. Maybe getting a cherry snow cone as the morning sun rose in the sky as the day grew warmer.

Every so often, at our elementary school, the PTA (Parent Teacher Association) would run a Saturday afternoon movie where the likes of *The Three Stooges*, *The Mummy*, *Dracula* could be seen all for a quarter or maybe fifty cents. And even once in a while, Big Chuck and Hoolihan (local TV celebrities who show monster movies on Friday nights on the local station) would bring movies with skits they've done and monster movies on 16 mm film.

As soon as you walked in, there were two long tables with penny candy. Yes, only a penny a piece got you Fireballs, Bull's Eyes, Tootsie Rolls, and such, even a stick pretzel or two. A box of popcorn and a pop rounded out our goodies for the movie.

We were like kings as we took a seat, being careful not to spill a drop of our goodies. As the room grew dark, you could hear the chatter of the film projector starting. As the screen lit up, our eyes grew wide as to see what was going to happen next as we shoved handfuls of popcorn and candy in our mouths, only stopping for a swallow of pop. Sometimes sinking in our seats, and yes, even closing our eyes at the scary parts.

The movie soon ended, and our candy was now gone. As we left the gym, we felt the sun warm on or faces. Sky was as blue as a robin's egg and not a cloud to be seen. As we walked out into the afternoon sun, we all laughed and said to each other, "I wasn't scared." Others saying, "Me neither."

As for me, well, maybe just a little—but don't tell them.

Yes, it's good to remember.

Guess you can say our past are like different pieces of cloth of a quilt. We cherish the good times and great people who touched our hearts.

But we also need to remember the bad times. When we got hurt, things that made us cry. People we lost and have gone home.

It makes us who we are today.

So always remember. Sure we're not kids anymore. But seems as we get older (like the Applewood gang), we're getting better-looking.

And lastly, as I've always said, "Behind every dark cloud is the sun just akin to come out and brighten our day."

Just sayin'.

Animal Crackers

Animal crackers. It's funny when you're a kid, imagination is your best friend. Well, next to your dog, of course. We can be astronauts going to the moon, cowboys being chased by Indians, and yes, even slaying dragons as they breathe fire at you. We seem to look at everything differently as we do as adults. Dogs are our new best friends. For one thing, they're our height. We got licks when we were happy and licks when we were sad.

One day, while chasing pirates, I tripped and cut my knee on a rock down by the stream. After my faithful friend ran off those scallywags (pirates to you, land lovers), she came over and licked my tears away. But this one time, she licked *so* hard, she almost licked my eyeball right out of my head. Boy, wonder what Mom would've thought? But I'm glad she didn't, though—who wants to be a pirate with a patch all the time?

It's amazing, as kids, we didn't have gigantic enormous—and I can't think of another word—big necks. When you're, small everything is bigger than you (except for your best friend). We're constantly looking up, our eyes seem to almost go into our eyebrows. When we need or want Mom or Dad for a drink, maybe a hug, or even some animal crackers. It's never easy being small. Yet when Mom picks you up, looks into those little eyes with that mom smile, and she tells you how much she loves you as she hugs you like a warm soft blanket, you forgot about being small for a while and just feel loved.

Just sayin'.

The Gift

In the early days of our grandparents, growing up on a farm during the Depression, There's wasn't a lot of money to be had. There were no cell phones or television but a radio next to the rocker in the living room. The kids would gather on the floor. Or maybe next to Mom on the couch. All wide-eyed, waiting in suspense to hear what was going to happen next on the radio. But it was family time after supper, and the kitchen was clean. They'd all sit and listen to the *Shadow* or some other show at the turn of the dial. Dad on his rocker, smoking his favorite pipe. Mom busy on the couch, mending holes in family socks and such. Always vigilant, like all moms, trying to make ends meet and last a little longer. And for a short time, their imagination transported them to far away places. Nothing like their lives living on the farm. Solving crimes with Charlie Chan in the Far East to shooting it out with Indians as you circle the wagons during an Indian attack, or even on a tall ship in the Seven Seas, being attacked by gigantic octopus.

Morning comes early on a farm. So as another chapter of the show comes to an end, and they soon sign off for the night. Tired from chores and playing hard, it's soon bedtime. It's not long after they say their prayers. They fall fast asleep not long after their heads hit the pillow. The dawning of the new day brings the familiar cry of the rooster, telling us time to get up. And as you wake, all snuggled close to you is old Blue, the hound dog, all curled up and warm next to you.

Soon it was Christmas time, and as kids do, they made their list of toys they wanted Santa to bring them. And every night, they dreamed of new dolls, wind-up locomotives, and yes, maybe a new baseball, as they fell fast asleep each night.

One night, after the kids went to sleep, Dad sat quietly smoking his pipe, sitting on his rocker, deep in thought. Worrying if Santa was going to make it to their house this year. Mom knew he was worried. You see, the kids were extra good, so they wouldn't be put on Santa's naughty list. She put her hand on his shoulder and said it will be okay. He looked up at her, all teary-eyed, nodded his head yes, as he reached for her hand.

With the tractor breaking down and the crops not doing as well as expected, they were just getting by, any extra money went into the farm to keep it running. Mom sold eggs from the farm. From that, she bought yarn, making scarves and mittens for the kids, wrapping them out of old brown paper bags and tinsel so the kids had something to open Christmas Day. She filled their stockings with new pairs of socks she made, an orange, and two cookies each. She made the cookies shaped as Christmas trees and candy canes. Mom and Dad finally went to bed late Christmas Eve. But Dad tossed and turned as no father wishes to disappoint his children. He couldn't sleep, so he decided to get up and get the chores done out in the barn.

He came back to the house, just as the kids were running around, opening their gifts, and eating Mom's cookies when he shouted, "Put on your coats and boots, Santa left one more present out in the barn." As they ran out there, their eyes widened and were all smiles. In front of them was the prettiest little colt you ever saw, newly born on this Christmas Day.

No, they didn't get a doll, a wind-up locomotive, or even a new baseball. But they didn't care, they had one another and loved the special present Santa left in the barn on this very special Christmas Day.

Just sayin'.

Hi, I Miss You

Hmmm, when you see a cardinal outside your window, it's said that it's a loved one from heaven, letting you know they're close by. Guess it makes us feel better. Maybe smile a little more, thinking of how much they love us. But there are those who think this belief is foolish. That when loved ones die—that's it.

It's a cynical world we live in. So many bad things are happening. We lose faith in ourselves as we stop believing in things we can't explain—unless it's right in front of us in black and white

And it's never easy to lose a loved one. The void caused by a death in our lives is like an open wound. It takes time, time to heal. And no, there's no set time in mourning a loved one.

It's a natural thing; we're born, we live, and we die. Pretty black and white, huh.

There's a saying, "to be able to see through a child's eyes," maybe we need to see lions, puppy dogs, and elephants in the clouds as they pass by. Or still believe in Santa Clause.

Then maybe people wouldn't laugh and say that's not true, or it's just a funny wise tale. Is it wrong to believe it's true? I don't think so. If it makes you happy and gives you peace, why not?

And to those who laugh and say it's foolish, I ask you this: do you believe in God? Have you seen him, how do you know he's real?

Guess everyone is entitled to their opinion. But if it gives you peace of mind, maybe make you smile, then God bless you—oh, and me, I still believe.

Just sayin'.

Hero

He's a hero, so few words can mean so much. A lot of us think of a hero as someone in the military who puts his life on the line to save others. And sometimes, they are wounded and may even become disabled. But no less a hero.

A loud scream for help from a burning building, "My god, please help us!"

A fireman risks his life to run into the burning building, hoping to save a life, not thinking of his own. With intense heat and parts of the building crashing down all around him, he soon emerges with a mother and her child. They quickly give oxygen to the mother and her baby. The mother looks up at the fireman from under the oxygen mask, looks into his eyes, and smiles at him, and then slowly closed her eyes, exhaling one last breath. The baby's color is coming back and crying like there's no tomorrow. He wraps the baby in a blanket and as he holds her, gently rocking her, his eyes well with tears. He lowers his head, asking God to watch over this little baby, whose mother went to him sooner than she wanted but protected her the best she could until she was safe.

You see, there are many ways to be a hero in someone's eyes. Heroes are all around us. Everyday people doing extraordinary things. A mother holding her little boy after he fell and scraped his knee. A boy's best friend, his dog, who licked away the tears when he fell out of the tree and slept by him to keep the monsters away. A man giving food to a homeless man. Holding the door for someone as you tell them good morning, or just listening and talking with someone who's lonely or elderly. Just everyday people doing extraordinary things.

God calls them angels. We call them heroes.
I kinda hope they're a little of both.
Just sayin'.

Dear Santa

Like all stories, we should start at the beginning. But we need to go way back, back before the letter to Santa that was written by little Jenny, in crayon.

It was a warm spring day in a little town by the river. Joseph was a good-looking young man who always had a smile on his face and always quick to say hello to you. He owned a small farm just outside of town. Well, one day, he drove his truck into town for supplies. He pulled in front of the hardware store. As he walked to the store, he accidently bumped into someone. He started to apologize, looked up, and froze. Standing before him was the most beautiful woman he'd ever seen. He just stared at her with a goofy smile. She started to laugh and told him, "Hi, I'm Mary. I just moved back home. I'm staying with my aunt and uncle, the Shepards on Third Street."

Now I'm telling you, she had the prettiest brown eyes and a smile that could light up a room. Well, you guessed it—he fell head over heels in love with her and soon married the love of his life.

Life on the farm wasn't always easy. But they always seemed to manage. Soon like a star from heaven, little Jenny was born. She grew fast and was as cute as could be. Soon Mom and Dad got her a pony. Now she could barely sit on the saddle, but she loved her pony. That pony would follow her around like a puppy dog; she would hug him and kiss him on the nose. And every once in a while, he would give kisses back, licking her face, making her giggle. Soon they were inseparable

What? The pony's name? Oh, I'm sorry, it's Cocoa. Jenny said because he looks like a chocolate bar.

Mom just smiled and said, "How about if we call him Cocoa?"

Jenny smiled as she hugged little Cocoa.

It was a happy time on the farm. That is, until one early December morning, Mary was running a fever and was sick to her stomach. The doctors at the hospital decided to admit her. They were puzzled and couldn't find what was wrong. She soon slipped into a coma. Weeks went by, Joseph stayed by Mary's side, praying to God, "Please don't take my Mary."

Back on the farm, Mary's aunt and uncle stayed with little Jenny. Soon it was Christmas Eve. Jenny was worried about her mom and didn't know what she could do. She took out a paper and a blue crayon and wrote:

> Dear Santa,
>   My mommy's very sick. You can keep all my toys I asked for. I'll even give you my pony, Cocoa, too if that will help. Please help Mommy feel better.
>
>   Jenny

Little Jenny folded the paper and wrote "SANTA" on the top and put it between his milk and cookies that she had put out for him. As she went to get ready for bed, the letter magically disappeared. Quickly it found its way to the North Pole to Santa. As he read the letter, he bowed his head. His eyes welled with tears, his heart grew heavy, and he wondered what he could do. This was beyond my magic. He thought for a moment. Then he said a prayer to God, telling him of the letter Jenny had written to him about her Mommy. He knew God must've heard. He felt the answer in his heart.

In the blink of an eye, it was Christmas Day. The phone rang; it's the hospital. Joseph answered the phone and began to cry. Mary was awake and asking for them. She soon recovered and was happily back home on the farm.

Oh, and Santa, he didn't forget about Jenny. She got everything she wanted in both letters with a little help, of course.

Just sayin'.

Just a Silver Dollar

Seems it was just like yesterday I was in high school. You see, back then, my parents gave us kids a silver dollar for a keepsake. Being the youngest, I think I was seventeen or eighteen years old. I was working for a grocery store (Fazio). When I was short on cash at work, I used it to buy a 16 oz. bottle of Pepsi using that silver dollar and asked the girls to put it in the safe till the next day, exchanging it with a dollar the next day. Needless to say, I did that quite a few times there. LOL.

Very few people ever knew I kept that silver dollar with me every day. No matter where I was or what I was doing, I didn't give it much thought. When I picked up my wallet and keys, I then picked up the silver dollar and put it in the little watch pocket in my jeans.

The silver dollar was to commemorate our country's birth, 1776–1976. They were called the Eisenhower dollar after President Eisenhower. Over the years, in my pocket, the little hair on his portrait has worn a little.

On the back was engraved the liberty bell and the moon. Two iconic events that helped shape our country.

Now you're probably wondering why the hell I'm telling you this.

Well, now guess it's twofold. For one, as a monetary value, it's still only worth a buck. But it reminds me of two people that I loved and respected. And when I look at it, I think of them and smile.

The other reason is that it has two distinct sides. Sometimes when I get mad at someone, I think back to how I was brought up. To not only see things from my point of view but maybe the other guy's too. And boy, that can be a hard thing to do at times.

Now I know some, if not all, are thinking, *Say it's not so, Bruce. How could this be that there would be times you'd be wrong?*

Well, sir, put your mind at ease because as you know, 99.9 percent of the time, I'm right. LMAO. But the coin, you see, is for that crazy 1 percent.

You see, to some it's just a coin. But as I get older, it reminds me to enjoy life a little more and to not sweat the small stuff.

Just sayin'.

Thanksgiving Day

We always look forward to this time of year. The gathering of good friends and family on Thanksgiving Day. There's nothing better than walking into the kitchen, the sight of fresh pies, fresh rolls, and such. But that smell that you waited all year for, your mouth waters just thinking of it. A golden-brown succulent turkey roasting in the oven.

And let's not forget the stuffing.

Well, now that I have your attention, there's a quote I remember. Goes like this, "There's three people we need in life. A doctor, a lawyer, and a farmer. The first two you need once, but a farmer you need three times a day for the rest of your life."

Growing up on a farm isn't as easy as you think. What with the weather and worrying about the health of the stock. Now I'm sure we all know, farmers raise their animals to sell for food. They grow grains for feed or to market for us to use. And sometimes to make ends meet, some even raise turkeys to sell at Thanksgiving. Like many, growing up on a farm, there's never shortage of chores to do.

On an early spring day, on a nearby farm, a truck pulled up to their barn. Just bursting full of young (baby) turkeys, and boy, what a racket they made. Soon they were unloaded. Dad had built a special area with heat lamps to keep them warm and said, "It's up to you to keep them fed and watered.

Young Johnny just nodded his head and said, "Okay, Dad."

Soon spring became summer, and the turkeys were so fat and sassy you couldn't even see their legs. They just kinda rolled side to side all day in the sunshine. That is, except when Johnny's dog, Bo, came running around the corner of the barn after them, tail wagging, barking at those turkeys. You see, old Bo was this big ole hound dog who just loved chasing those turkeys. Well, I'll tell you, what a sight that was. Them turkeys took one look at Bo coming at them, and all I saw was white blurs with legs going by me like a freight train. Feathers flying, turkeys saying, "For god's sake, Bo's loose again," (in turkey language, of course). Running for the barn, once inside, Bo stopped the chase; he had his fun. And eventually lay on the warm grass and took a nap.

Soon summer turned to fall. It was time for the turkeys to go to market. It's not easy for a young boy, growing up on a farm, not to get attached to all the animals. Some are pets, but some are raised to sell to help keep the farm running. Dad said the truck would be there Saturday to take the turkeys. He noticed all week that Johnny was spending a lot of time in the barn with them, just sorta talking to them and petting their feathers.

Well, before you knew it, Saturday was here. The whole family helped load all of the turkeys into the truck. Dad noticed that Johnny was kinda quiet. Being a dad isn't always easy. Especially a dad on a farm where it's business. He teared up looking at his son and took a step back. A small smile came on his face. You see, no parent wants to see his kids hurting. But he was also proud of his son. This is a part of being a farmer on a farm. Raising animals, taking care of them until market time, and then selling them off. He knew Johnny was learning his part to becoming a good farmer.

As for Johnny and Bo, just a few weeks later, it was Thanksgiving. Mom made one of the best Thanksgiving dinners you ever saw. With turkey and ham, mash potatoes, fresh rolls, and three kinds of pies! She even made Bo a special dinner. Like all good friends, bellies full and fast asleep, lying together on a rug in front of the fireplace, all nice and warm. And Dad, well, he looked over at those two and just smiled—you know, that Dad smile—at the little farmer and Bo.

Just sayin'.

Sorry, Not My Problem

Seems being the last of the baby boomers, we laugh and joke how good we had it back then. But as we got older, our parents would tell us stories of how money was tight at times. And they needed to economize the best they could.

For example, we would go to the drive-in. We'd see some cartoons and a movie. Played on the swings. Mom packed a picnic basket of sandwiches and such. We even popped a big bag of popcorn with lots of butter. And ice-cold bottles of Pepsi.

We were kings—okay, so we thought. But to our parents, it saved money when money seemed a little tight back then.

Today's families face even harsher realities. With many good-paying jobs long gone or moved overseas, the struggle to survive even with two paychecks is hard. But even harder when you can't put food on your table. When you're forced to make harsh decisions.

What bills get paid and will there be any leftover to feed my babies? A mother's prayer at night, asking God for guidance. Tears roll down her face in the darkness as she lies there in bed, not knowing what to do; and in the morning, she knows there's not much for her children to eat before school. It hurts her so when she hears them say to her, "Mommy, I'm still hungry."

She's crushed, but she fights back the tears as she says, "Better get going, you'll be late for school." She gives them a hug and a kiss and says I love you.

The city schools' budgets, like many municipalities, are tight. Some offer a little breakfast in the morning before classes. For it's hard to concentrate when your little belly aches from not eating.

Many kids go without eating because no money is put in their lunch account. Lunch ladies are forced by their bosses to say, "I'm sorry, you can't have lunch today because you don't have money." All the while as adults and students watch on. They hold back their tears, heads down, and quietly go sit till the lunch period is over.

Some lunch ladies pay out of their own pockets only to realize it's against the school policy and are let go. Other school systems believe that no child should go without eating programs. They give them a cheese sandwich. But that too falls short. For the other students know the kids who get a cheese sandwich are poor and don't have money.

Our children are our future.

As a whole, we need to take better care of our children. I've heard of states who have passed a law that all children will be fed a regular lunch every day whether they have money or not.

Why isn't it in every state of the union? Our children are our future. Our poets, our teachers, our scientists. And yes, our dreamer. For if you can't imagine it, how can you do it?

Just sayin'.

Going Home

They say you can never go home again. Seems the older we get, we cherish the days of our youth. Yes, they were simpler times. We played from morning to way in the dark. We built forts in the woods and even made slingshots from hickory tree branches.

Yes, it was a simpler time, and a shame kids today don't get to enjoy what we did. Where we had to look up things at the library. In a blink of an eye, kids can surf the net on their phones or computer.

Kindles allow us to read any book in the world just by downloading it from a list of books on the Internet. Me, maybe I'm a throwback, showing my age. But I still like the feel and smell of a book in my hands. And did you ever try to lick and turn the pages on a Kindle? Very messy, and they make fun of you.

It's been a long road from our youth. We will always remember fondly of the neighborhood kids. And all the good times we shared. Like our parents and the parents in every generation, we tell our kids how good they have it. And how things weren't so easy when we were their age.

But as for me, I don't think I'd change anything. Sure, as we get older we fondly remember the good times and slowly forget the not-so-good times. Like a never-ending book, we make new friends and, yes, even fall in love.

But all those things are like a patch quilt. It's who we are. Sure, we're a little more gray, maybe some wrinkles, and yes, maybe a pound or two heavier than our youth. Yet deep inside is that kid from the old neighborhood.

Yes, I guess it's true we can't go back to our youth. Seems we've grown too much. But we can remember and share with our friends as we laugh and reminisce about the days of our youth.

That is till we all go home.

Just sayin'.

What Did We Learn?

We are born into this world kicking and screaming. Yes, letting everyone know we're here. Just like generations before us, wide-eyed and eager to learn. At first, taking baby steps, new to learning. A far cry from being protected in our mother's womb as we learn to sit up or take our first steps, learning about all these strange new things around us.

As we grow, we constantly learn, and we remember. Like that big fury thing that always made my face wet as I was learning to walk and sometimes fell. And who was always there when I was scared and maybe cried.

As I grew and learned, I learned that it was our dog—and also my best friend.

Soon in a blink of an eye, we have families of our own. We smile as we hold that bundle of joy. All the while laughing inside that if she's her father's daughter, she'll be a handful. But she'll learn, just as we did. Just one step at a time, always watching, always learning. And just as she will be with her little boy.

Seems now she's all grown-up with a family of her own. A little older but always learning.

As for me, seems I'm a little older. A few more wrinkles and a little grayer maybe. Yet each day, there still seems something I can learn. Like there's nothing better than the giggle of a small child, a nice glass of good sipping whiskey, and the love of a good woman. Yet of all the things I've learned in my humble life, the one I cherish the most is that I'm never alone. That God is always with me. Guess we never stop learning till the day we die.

So how about you? What have you learned today?

Just sayin'.

Easter Morning in My Little Town

Well, now, it sure is a beautiful Easter morning here in my little town. Sun's coming up over the horizon. Feeling so warm on my face and the air smelling so fresh and sweet.

A gentle breeze blows through the red bud trees as they're just starting to bloom. Soon the trees will be full of deep-pink trumpet-shaped flowers. Yet just another sign, letting us know it's spring, and summer's not far behind.

An assortment of songbirds perched on its branches. Seem to do a little dance as the wind blows through the trees. All the while singing their beautiful songs. And if you look close, you might even see a pair of cardinals. Well, that's another story.

Soon the sound of church bells can be heard as they call out, "It's time for meeting and to give thanks," on this Easter Sunday.

But I'm getting a little ahead of myself here.

Our police and fire stations have been getting swamped with calls from all over town. Seemed late last night as our children slept, parents were hearing a rustling in the bushes and a funny sound.

"Now I know it's going to sound crazy..." said one parent. "But it sounded like someone hopping around. And every once in a while, a crunching sound."

Soon all through the neighborhood, you could see flashlights going off in the darkness. Like fireflies in the dark night as parents wondered what it was. And finally—

One of the dad's shouted out, "I found something!"

Well, I'm telling you, they all came a running into Mark's yard to see what the commotion was about. And lo and behold, there in the dirt, by the missus' roses—were two big rabbit footprints and a half-eaten carrot on the ground next to them.

Soon as other parents came up to see just what it was in our bushes, making that funny sound, they let out a sigh of relief and soon a smile came across their faces as if they heard someone say, "Well, bless my soul…it's just Peter Cottontail (the Easter bunny), just makin' his rounds."

Hopping around our neighborhood, delivering the Easter baskets for all the kids. Just bursting with candy-colored eggs and such. You know, carrying those baskets to each and every house has got to make any rabbit hungry. Guess I'd be munching on a few carrots myself.

Come Easter Sunday, the kids jump out of bed. All wide-eyed to see where the Easter bunny hid their basket. Until—"I found it! I found it! I found my Easter basket!"

Mom and dad just smiled, thinking of what happened last night.

Well, seems I'm burning daylight and almost out of coffee. So I better get movin'. But I'd like to leave you with this one thought.

Teach your children the true meaning of Easter. And how he has risen for us. And learn from our children not to always be so serious. For there was a time when Peter Cottontail brought us an Easter basket full of candy and toys and such. Just sayin'.

Fear

Believe it or not, we all fear something. How we handle fear is twofold. One is head-on, and, of course, the other—well, we avoid it and go about our business. That is, unless it crosses our path once more.

At this point, your mind is starting to wonder, what are some of the things I've a fear of? Some are big and some are small. Both can give you the willies and just make you shudder.

Like now, do you feel something as you read this? Maybe like an itch on your neck. You know, like a spider crawling up. You feel each leg as it touches your neck. Almost in your hair—you scream as you try and swat it away. Not knowing what it is. And then you see it, quickly stomping it to smithereens.

OMG, that was close.

We've had fun talking of small fears, but some aren't so fun. There are many we fear, like the fear of heights or losing a loved one. The fear of being alone, or yes, maybe drowning. These make our hearts race, we pull back, we don't know what to do—we're scared.

Whatever you fear, if it affects your life, don't let it run your life. Face it, maybe a little at a time, baby steps.

For example, I used to go white-water rafting and told people trust your equipment and keep your head—don't panic. So if you fall back in four feet of water with a life jacket on, it will keep you up. If you don't panic, you'll be able to handle a situation if it occurs. If you panic, you could drown. And we'll find you downriver maybe because you wore your life jacket.

Oh and me, I don't swim. I'd almost drowned as a kid. It's a fear I've dealt with. I respect the water. Sure, that fear is always with me in the back of my mind. But I don't let it control me. Instead I enjoy gliding over the water.

Don't let fear control you. If you have a fear, and it controls you, you're not living; and if you haven't noticed, it's a beautiful world out there. Face your fears one step at a time.

Now I'm far from perfect, and I don't know everything. But sometimes, I, at least, hope that I made you smile. Maybe made you think and, yes, even belly laughed at something I wrote.

Well, I'm burning daylight and just about out of coffee. So I hope I made you think and hope you enjoy this day.

Just sayin'.

One More Look at You

Guess it's something we don't always talk about. That is, losing someone we loved. It's never easy as we go through an emotional roller-coaster ride. Thinking of them and times we shared. All the times you laughed until you cried. And held them when they hurt. Letting them know you're here.

Try as you will, at times, we lose track of time itself. With this and that, and now the weather. It's not that we don't love them or don't want to spend time with them. We just get busy with work and our families.

We wish and pray for just one more look at them. To see their smile, to hear that laugh—to say I love you and just how much you mean to me.

It seems the older we get, life seems to take back more than she gives us. We're happy they've gone home and aren't in any more pain. But our hearts hang heavy, knowing we won't see them till it's our time to go home. But for now, their love and memories are kept in that special place loved ones are kept—close to our heart and in our thoughts.

Just sayin'.

The North Coast

Sure looks like another beautiful day. Sky so blue, sun so bright. Going up to near sixty today. Guess that's not too bad for late February.

But we live up on the North Coast where anything is possible. Sure it's not 80 degrees, like our friends in Florida. But we always look at the bright side of things.

So let's get those sunglasses on. Maybe get the grills fired up. And if you listen close, you'll hear the rumble of motorcycle riders. Eager to feel the wind in their face and enjoy riding the first ride since late fall.

For all you polar bears, who jump in the lake for charity this time of year, again God bless you. I feel bad, once more, I lost the address to your event. Or I'd be jumping in the ice-cold numbing water with you on this beautiful yet warm winter's day.

But rest assured, I'll be there in spirt with you all as you take that lake plunge. For as I start up the grill and barbecue today with my sunglasses on, sun warm on my face, and when they ask if I want a cold drink, I'll answer, "Yes, sir, and plenty of ice."

Well, I'm burning daylight, better get going. But I'll leave you with just a thought. Life is short, make the best of it. For behind every storm is the sun just akin to shine down on you.

Just sayin'.

Wellington's Beauty in the Fall

Just another beautiful day in my little town of Wellington.

I don't think it could get any prettier, at least until tomorrow.

The sky's so blue, and the sun's so warm on your face. There's a gentle cool breeze, reminding us that winter will soon be here.

Farmers are busy in their fields, bringing in their crops before the winter snow. They sit high in their combines that cut the pale yellow dried stalks of corn in their fields, separating the corn from the stalks. The now-dried kernels of corn, just pulled up by a farm hand, are ready to fill large trucks.

That will, in turn, fill the silos on the farm for feed for their animals or to be sold at the market.

In the far distance, close to the woods, a few deer are eating the leftover corn in the field that the farmer missed. The young does are prancing around like little kids, but they always take care and stay close to their mom.

A group of Canadian geese fly overhead in their perfect V-formation, letting us know that they are around by honking as they fly by.

And in the background of all of this, the trees in the woods, so tall they seem to touch the sky. Yet they almost look like they are on fire. With the leaves just bursting with colors so bright. Reds, yellows, oranges, and browns. Colors so beautiful it would make an artist blush.

Yes, this is my little piece of America.

We're not perfect.

But we're always glad you stopped by.

Well, you guessed it. Once more, I'm burning daylight and better get a move on. And that coffee cup must have a hole in it 'cause it's empty again. Better fill it before I go out.

One final thought. Take a second out of your busy day, say good morning to someone, hold a door open for them, watch their face light up and say thank you. And if they don't. You could kinda trip them going out the door. Just remember to wish them a nice day.

Just sayin'.

Sunday Morning in My Little Town

Well, now it sure is a beautiful morning here in my little town of Wellington. Warm sun on my face. Birds are singing, letting us know spring's just around the bend.

For those getting ready for church. Better hurry, you don't want to be late, might be a good sermon today. For the rest of us, it's time for another cup of coffee. Maybe some toast with homemade jam as we read the funny pages in our pj's.

Always makes me smile when I hear the church bells in the distance. Letting people know it's time to give thanks after another week. And reminding me that God is always near and happy to listen if I need him. Sometimes I remember the hymns the bells sing out from the church tower that we sang as kids in our little church. Those great times will always be with me.

You see, memories are great to share with others. But what's even better is building new memories with the ones you love.

Well, seems once more, my coffee cup is getting low, and I'm burning daylight. So I better let you go. Hope you get to enjoy this beautiful day.

Just sayin'.

Mom's Pot Roast

Well, it's Sunday morning in my little town of Wellington. Sun's just coming up to start the new day. Morning air is a little cool, the dew heavy on the grass. And a good cup of coffee tastes good as it warms my hands. All the while sitting on the patio as the new day unfolds.

Sun feels good on my face as I start to hear the songbirds sing their first songs of the day. As if to say, "Good morning, it's time to get up." And in the distance, you can hear the whistle of a train as it grows close to our town. As the engineer blows his whistle, letting us know he's near. As it passes through, delivering its goods to its destination.

Soon the church bells will ring out. Letting us know it's time for meeting and give thanks to God. All dressed in their Sunday best, a young family walks into church. Shaking hands, saying hello to good friends. As Mom and Dad file the kids one by one into the pew for the service. Halfway through the service, the kids get fidgety. But one stern look from Mom, and they seem to turn into little angels once more. Dad's trying to pay attention to the minister's sermon. All the while thinking of how good his wife's pot roast is going to taste when they get home.

Well, seems I'm burning daylight and just about out of coffee. I hope you enjoyed hearing just a little bit of my little town. Wanted to write a little more. But I hear my old friend (my kayak) calling me. LOL, whispering in my ear, saying it's a beautiful morning. The lake is like glass, let's go play.

Just sayin'.

Barb, the Mayor

Well now, it looks to be another beautiful fall day in my little town of Wellington. It's November 3, and it looks like we're in for some late Indian summer. For many of the trees, the leaves have fallen are now bare, yet there's still trees bursting full of colors of deep red, golden yellow, and of course, russet browns. Guess mostly their hardwood trees, they seem to hold on till the first snow, if not till spring.

Today, like many towns, it's voting day. It's kinda bittersweet, a changing of the guards, so to speak.

Barb, the mayor, after about twenty-three years has decided to step down. But what a legacy she leaves and is leaving on a high note. A new middle school is to open after Thanksgiving break as well as a new underpass that will keep Route 58 open through all the train traffic going through town. A very smart businesswoman who always took time for you. But for me, I'll miss her smile, and she was always glad to see you. During a parade, I'd be on my front porch on my rocker, and I'd hear, "Hey, Bruce," yelled from an antique car passing by. Waving and smiling away was Barb, the mayor.

And I'd yell back, "Hi, Barb!" And smile. I'll miss her as our mayor. But I consider myself lucky to still call her my neighbor as well as my friend. Seems like our little town is growing up, just like a child. As much as we would like to keep them small, all we can do is guide them and hope for the best.

But for now, why not pull up a chair, come sit for a while, coffee's just about ready.

Just sayin'.

Hey, God, I'm Glad You're Here

It's funny, as we get older, we start to realize that we're never alone. That if we know it or not, God is always near if we need him. Seems a lot of times, we talk to him out loud. Yet many times, we, so to speak, turn the volume down to just between God and I.

He doesn't mind that we pray and ask him to be with a friend or family member who's sick or who said goodbye to a loved one's gone home.

He always listens.

When you're scared and not sure, he's always there. Sometimes we know deep down. Yet at times, he only asks that we keep the faith and believe in him.

Our belief in God is sometimes as different as pages in a book. All different, yet when we all come together, we seem to come together as one, as in our God.

Faith is a fickle friend we go to in times of trouble. When we're scared and frustrated and don't know what else to do. It's said that we're made in his image, yet we're only human.

We sometimes fall, not always making the right decisions. But like our father, he's right there. To pick us up, brush us off. Maybe wipe away our tears. As he looks down at us and smiles as we try once again.

I can only hope I made you smile a little, reading these simple words. Maybe made you think just a little. And eased your mind just a little.

That you're never alone.

Just sayin'.

Just a Walk in the Park

It was a beautiful spring day. Sun so bright, you'd swear it could light up all creation. And the sky, well, as blue as a robin's egg. Me, I grabbed a cup of coffee and decided to take a walk along the river's bank. The trees were just about to burst open as the warm sun shined down upon them. As the daffodils dotted the river's bank, letting us know winter's now gone, and spring is finally here.

The sun was warm on my face, and the air smelled so fresh. I was enjoying my walk along the river when I came upon an elderly man sitting on a park bench. You see, he caught my attention as I was walking by. He looked like he was deep in thought. But as I got closer, our eyes met, and a slow grin came upon his face as he said good morning.

I smiled and said, "Yes, it is."

He said, "Would you like to have a seat?"

I said, "Sure."

"By the way, my name is Joe."

I said, "It's nice to meet you, I'm Butch." We slowly began to talk as people walked by.

Joe was an elderly man leaning toward eighty, I think. But I knew better than to ask. He wore a dark-blue three-piece suit. His shoes were smartly shined. As he leaned forward a little, leaning on his walking stick, though I don't think he needed it for support. It was a stylish mahogany stick with a silver top and a tiger eye stone on the top. I mentioned it's a beautiful walking stick. A slow smile came upon him as his eyes welled just little. He said, "My late wife, Gracie, gave me that on my last birthday. Sadly she went home last fall to heaven."

I said, "I'm sorry for your loss, Joe. She must've been a great lady."

He said, "Yes, she was. I feel the closest to her down here. But she's always with me."

I sat there, listening to him, and watched as his weathered face lit up as he told me of the love his life.

Turned out this was their favorite spot. And in fact, he proposed to her right here. He told me how much he was in love with her. How he had this planned for so long. "So I knelt down on one knee as she sat on the bench in front of me. On a warm spring day such as this one."

He stopped for a moment. I said, "Well, what did she say?"

His eyes welled, and a smile as big as Texas came over his face as he told me, "She said *yes*! Now that was pretty close to fifty years ago."

Well it's hard to believe, but we seemed to talk the whole afternoon. He told me, "Well, I'm burning daylight. I best be getting back home." As he got up, I shook his hand and thanked him. He said, "For what?"

I said, "For telling me about your Gracie and how much you truly loved her."

He just smiled and said, "It was my pleasure," and said, "Good day to you."

Sir.

I sat back down on the bench as I watched him walk away. Steady as an oak tree as he strutted with his cane Gracie had given him.

I thought to myself how lucky I was to be walking down by the river on this fine spring day and met Joe. And on this very bench, a young couple fell in love. And how a young man, full of butterflies, finally got the nerve to ask for her hand. And the rest is history, I guess.

Well, guess like Joe, I'm burning daylight too. Best be going. For some reason, I walked down by the river's edge. Leaning against tree, watching the river pass by me.

As I started to leave, I noticed something on the bark of the tree. You could still make it out. A heart with an arrow going through it. And in that heart read, "Joe loves Gracie...4 ever."

As I touched it, I just grinned as I walked away.

Coincidence, hmmm, guess that's something for you to decide. Just sayin'.

Will You?

He looked at his watch, it's 11:59 p.m. His mind, somewhat weary, it's been a long day. He'd been thinking long and hard about things. But one thing in particular. as he gently held her hand in his. As he sat next to her, thinking about it over and over.

Sorry, maybe I'm getting ahead of myself a little.

Let me introduce you to some friends of mine, George and Gracie. Nicest couple you'll ever want to meet.

They live in the little white house on the corner next to me. With the white picket fence and the prettiest pink rose garden you'll ever see. And even in the gentlest of breeze, you can smell Gracie's sweet-smelling roses.

Gracie was very soft-spoken Southern lady who always had a smile on her face and a twinkle in her eye when she talked about George. On this particular day, it happened to be Sunday. She had walked out in the garden as she was waiting for George to come out so they could walk down to church service.

A true Southern older lady, her hair now as white as pure driven snow, all done up in a do, wearing a beautiful blue dress that George got her for her last birthday.

Well, seemed George finally came out. All dressed in his Sunday best suit, grumbling like an old bear 'cause he couldn't get that darn tie tied up. "And, Gracie, how about me just not wearing one today, just this once."

She scolded him, saying, "You can't go to church half-dressed." She gave him stern look as she did his tie.

A slow smile came on George as he said, "You know, Gracie, you sure do look pretty in that blue dress."

She just smiled and said, "I love you too. Now let's get going so we're not late for service."

Well, now looked like the preacher was on a roll. Seemed he was really getting into the sermon. Guess George thought he was getting a little long-winded. And when Gracie wasn't looking, he gave the preacher the let's-wrap-it-up-and-bring-it-on-home signal. He just smiled at George with a little nod and brought it home, so to speak.

As they walked out, old George shook the minister's hand as he said, "Really loved the sermon today," as Gracie agreed.

The preacher just smiled at George as he looked him in the eye and said, "I'm glad you enjoyed it."

It was just another beautiful Sunday morning here in the South. As Gracie and George walked back home, holding hands. Gracie, telling George, "Looks like it's going to be another pretty day."

He said, "I think you're right, Gracie."

They stopped for a moment as Grace took her lace handkerchief out of her purse. And wiped her forehead, and then she grabbed her chest. George gently laid her on the grass as he cried out for help. "Somebody, please help us!" He took off his best jacket and gently folded it under Gracie's head. "It's okay, Grace...I'm right here. Help is coming," as he held her hand. He shouted once more, "Please, somebody help us, *please help my Gracie!*"

Well, now, don't fret too much. The ambulance came and got Gracie to the hospital. As George picked up his coat, something fell out of his coat pocket. He put his coat back on and put it back in his pocket.

Turned out, it was Grace's heart. George sat there in the waiting room. You could hear a pin drop. Staring down at the floor, thinking how lucky he's been, being married to grace. Just then, his friend, the church preacher, walked in. Gave him a hug, said he just heard about Gracie and came as soon as he could. "I said a prayer for Grace on the way over here."

George said, "I know, I've been talking to God too."

The doctor finally came out, said that Grace would be fine, so he could see her now. She's in her room now. As he walked in, there were so many wires to monitors, and she was on oxygen.

His eyes welled with tears as he asked God to please don't take his Gracie. He sat on the chair next to her bed, all the while holding her hand. He wouldn't leave her side. It was such a long day. As day turned to night, he thought of his life together with Gracie. He looked at his watch—11:59 p.m.—all the while muttering to himself, "Gracie, will you? Gracie, would you?"

Just then, Gracie woke up. She pushed the oxygen mask off her face for a moment.

"Will I what, George!"

Tears rolled down his cheeks. "I missed you so, please don't ever leave me again. I love you, Gracie."

A smile came across her as her eyes welled with tears as she said, "I love you, George, and I'll always be here."

She then asked, "While I was sleeping, I could hear your voice asking me something, 'Will you?'"

A slow smile came across his face as he looked at his watch. "It's 12:05 a.m.," he said.

"So..." she said.

He reached in his right coat pocket and pulled out a now-tattered red envelope. Puzzled, she said, "What is that?"

As he handed it to her, he whispered in her ear, "Gracie. I love you to the moon and back. Will you be my valentine?"

Well, now you know she said yes.

Gracie got better and went home. Things seemed to get back to normal. George still has trouble with that darn tie. Seems Gracie doesn't mind tying the tie anymore. Even when George tries to fish for a kiss afterward.

Oh, and if you ever get a chance to visit George and Gracie's house, there up on the mantle, sits a beat-up old valentine's card with lace that reads:

> To the moon and back
> I love you, Gracie!
> Happy Valentine's Day

Just sayin'.

Daddy's Hands

It seems so long ago, yet I can remember it like it was yesterday. You see, your mom and I weren't married very long. We didn't have much money back then. Just being married and starting a new life together.

But I was so much in love with your mom. Nothing was impossible because she believed in me as I did with her.

It was a warm summer evening, after supper. We sat out on the back porch on the swing, listening to the crickets. A big ole moon was just hanging out with a sky full of stars. And me, I was fishing for a kiss from your mom. She finally gave in and kissed me. And then asked me, "Babe, remember when we were kids, and we'd make a wish upon a star?" Well, before I could answer her, she took me by the hand and said, "Come on," as we walked out into the backyard. Looking up at a sky full of stars, she said, "Let's make a wish."

I just nodded my head and smiled as I said okay.

> Star light
> Star bright
> First star I see tonight
> I wish I may
> I wish I might
> Make this wish
> I wish tonight…

All of a sudden, your mom had a smile as big as Texas on her face. I said, "Okay, what's going on?"

"Did you make a wish?" she asked.

I said, "Yes, I wished for a new truck!"

A slow smile came over her face as she looked up at me. She asked, "Would you be disappointed if you didn't get a truck but something else?" I just smiled and said sure.

She said, "Honey, I'm pregnant."

I was so happy and gave your mom a big hug and kiss.

Well, your mom had a hard pregnancy and ended up having you a little earlier than expected. We almost lost your mom in the delivery. But she pulled through just fine.

And you, you were so tiny and frail in that little incubator. I never told your mom about the first time I saw you. I was so scared as I walked up to see you in the incubator, connected with all those wires. I just teared up; you were so small and fragile, lying there. So small you could fit in one of my hands. I prayed to God to please protect you and be with you and your mom. I felt helpless, nothing I could do but trust in the doctors and, of course, God.

But turned out, you were a fighter. Soon you gained weight, and you had the nurses all fighting over you as you smiled and seemed to try and talk to them.

And then—

I got to hold you for the first time in my hands. You looked so small and frail in my big weathered hands. My eyes welled as I looked down at you. As I said to you, "Hello, son, I'm your daddy, and I love you so much." You got a grin on you as big as Texas—well, almost.

And you seemed to talk back to me, as if to say, Hi, Daddy, it's nice to finally meet you."

Well, now seems you've grown into a great young man. And your mom and I have always been proud of you. And for that matter, always will. I think back so many years ago as I saw you hold your newborn son for the first time. It's a great bond between a father and son that I hope will last a lifetime.

The first time you hold your son in Daddy's hands.

Just sayin'.

One Last Ride

I don't think you'll see a prettier fall morning in my little town of Wellington. At least not until tomorrow. Sun so bright, it seems to make the surrounding landscape just bust wide open in color. Many of the houses already decorated in skeletons, ghosts, and flying witches. Why, I even saw Frankenstein and the wolfman just hanging down the street. All waiting patiently for the little ghouls and goblins on Halloween night, as they run from house to house, screaming trick or treat all through the neighborhood. All the while stuffing their bags full of candy.

My dad used to say, "The sun's a fooler," this time of year. Meaning the sun is warm on your face, but the air is cool. Reminding us winter's not far behind. But like everyone else, I hope we still get Indian summer. One more time in my kayak on the lake before it's put away for the winter. There's something magical about being on the lake this time of year. The way the sun shines down, making the lake glisten. The way the trees, so full of color, mirror themselves all around the lake. A group of Canadian geese fly over, honking, letting us know they're still here. The blue herring have gone, most likely have flown South for the winter. Yet there's a peace you get gliding over the water. Seeing all the fall colors and watching some of the animals as they get ready for a long winter's nap. And inside, I chuckle, remembering a friend asking me when they heard I was going kayaking, "Isn't the water cold?"

I'd smile and say, "Only if you fall in."

Well, I better get going. I'm burning daylight, just about out of coffee. And always remember, an act of kindness only takes a moment but could last a lifetime.

Just sayin'.

Deaf, Dumb, and Blind

I grow angry when I see and hear in the news how cemetery graves and statues of white people from the Civil War are removed from Southern cities because liberals and blacks find it so offensive in their modern daily lives.

I live in an area where slaves from the South were smuggled out through the underground railway. Hidden in houses, in basements and barns of good people, both black and white. Feeding, clothing, and protecting them from harm until they can continue their journey to freedom. Who believed, just as their president did, that all men are created equal.

Let's let that sink in a little—*all men are created equal.*

That does not put black people's rights above white people's rights. If you look through history, there's many atrocities through history that shows all races, at one time or another, have seen bigotry and, yes, slavery. I've read in some books how white people fought and died to protect and defend the rights of slaves. Yet to my knowledge, there's no statue of a white person in all these underground railroad remembrances.

In my surrounding community, there are statues of Martin Luther King. A man who believed in civil rights. When he marched, he made his point through words—good words. Not like black groups today (BLM) who think it's okay to burn, pillage, and destroy to make their point.

Many innocent people have died because they were white, or people who didn't follow the beliefs of these black groups.

Why are people deaf to their cries, their deaths? Why do they look away and blindly not see that violence solves nothing? Guess that's just dumb, huh.

There are many statues of the underground railroad and black slavery in our area. Many federal funded. Hmm, is the money segregated? I mean do you just use black people's money or white people's too? To make your point and further your cause? I'm sure you don't care. To want your belief, respected you must respect others as well equally.

I don't think I need a crystal ball to know that if I got a lawyer and filed a lawsuit against the city that I find the statue of Martin Luther King in the city limits, racist and very offensive against white people. Pretty sure we'd be on national news. Every black person would be up in arms, civil right groups from around the country would flock here to protest.

But you ask, "Why they would do that?"

Just maybe he's a large part of black history!

And the civil rights movement. To remember, and yes, to learn from that part of history, what has happened in the past and learn from it.

During WWII, in Nazi Germany, they'd have big propaganda gatherings and burned books. Many German people helplessly stood by and cried, who were there. Refugees, far from home, in disbelief. How could they destroy our history and source of knowledge?

Like a pebble rolling down a hill, it starts to snowball and can't stop.

When we start to remove our history like statues, graves, and even books, we limit ourselves to learn. Not only to learn from our past but also likely make the same mistakes again and again.

We can't always change things to suit us or our causes. It's part of who we are. We learn from our past and hope to better our future.

And if we don't learn and change, we become deaf, dumb, and blind.

Just sayin'.

That special love

To a newborn baby, to your first love, to the little blond blue-eyed girl down the street, or that moment when you fell down and skinned your knee. There was only one person to make it feel all better. It was almost magical. Being held in your mom's arms, cradled against her body, kissing you gently, softly telling you, "It's okay, I'm right here."

Even a boy's best friend, his dog, who stood by him through thick and thin. Who's always protected him from harm, and yes, shared his peanut butter and jelly sandwiches that Mom made just for them, and yes, his tears.

You see, your heart isn't just an organ pumping blood. It's also full of love. That warm fuzzy feeling you got when you first fell in love with your high school sweetheart to coming home after a hard day. Your wife's been cooking, cleaning, chasing kids all day. She's a wreck. You look into her eyes and realize how lucky you are. Okay, actually you think the house looks like a cyclone went through it. She could've gotten out of the bathrobe and at least pulled her hair back into a ponytail! But instead you keep quiet 'cause you're hungry, and you know better.

Have you ever watched an old couple? Sometimes we forget they were once our age, and sooner than later, we'll be theirs. Sure they might not be too stable at times or see so well anymore. All wrinkly and walk with a cane, but when he looks into her eyes, there's still magic there. He looks at her with that special little smile and twinkle in his eyes. He sees that young girl he fell head over heels in love with so many long years ago. He smiles as he gently holds her hand. And then she turns and looks at him and says in a loud voice, *"What did you say?"*

"Oh, for god's sake, Ethel, turn on your hearing aid!"

Well, sir, she did just that, and he told her again. Her eyes filled with tears as she held him and said, "To the moon and back, I love you too."

Guess we're never too old to tell someone I love you.

Whoever it may be, you never know, they just might smile and say it back to you. And for those that we will always love, who have died or moved on, there will always be that special place in our hearts where loved ones go. Their memories keep us warm and full of smiles.

Well, I'm burning daylight, and as always, another cup of coffee sounds good. Just sayin'.

Excuse me

I just had a ARRP member moment.

I looked at the right top of my phone and thought it was 75 degrees out but had to laugh. I Just realized I still have 75 percent of my battery left to make fun of myself.

Oh, and in case you're still wondering, it's a balmy 66 degrees out, and now 71 percent of my battery to make fun of myself.

On a lighter side, opened all the windows, let out all that winter stink. Smells like a spring day.

And now I've got 70 percent of my battery to make fun of myself.

Well, now seems I'm burning daylight, better get moving. Enjoy this beautiful warm day in February. Have to go plug my phone into the charger.

Just sayin'.

Applewood Gang

Now I ask you, did you ever see a prettier morning?

I look out the window as I sip my cup of coffee. A slow smile comes across my face. As I think of my friends I grew up with, called the Applewood gang.

As birthdays come and go for us all, I still see the faces of my friends of my youth. There are some that say we can never go back. And that may be true. But they will always be close to my heart and so cherished.

And as years passed, I like to think we're not getting older, just better-looking. The kids called the Applewood gang.

Just sayin'.

What a Friend We Have

It's funny how a song can trigger a memory. Years ago, we were building high-end condos in little Italy. And they were going to do a charity auction in the model condo.

My boss asked if I'd help bring in some of the artwork that arrived. And since I worked for him, I said sure. Now the woman who was in charge of it was a buxom blond beauty with curves in all the right places, long blond hair, and had such beautiful—hello. And all nestled in between was a cross on a fine chain around her neck.

As we unloaded the SUV, I picked up a box. And as I turned, my eyes were looking right at the cross—kinda mesmerized me. I couldn't look away; I just smiled. I looked upon that cross, all comfortable where it was. And all I could think of was a song from my childhood.

"What a friend we have in Jesus."

And in my head, singing the first line, all the while smiling. She caught me looking her way.

She smiled and said, "Are you done?" as she laughed.

I said, "I guess," as I blushed.

We finished getting things ready. She smiled as she thanked me and with a wink as she walked away.

So whenever I hear that song, I smile a little more because yes, I have another friend in Jesus. LMAO

I feel so bad, bahahaha.

Just sayin'.

Northwinds

Well, it looks like after yesterday's big blow (high winds), it's finally starting to look a little more like winter. Gone are the last of the beautiful fall leaves of the trees. Warm sun on your face, and lastly, the smell of fresh-cut grass. The now-bare trees against a gray November sky.

Seem more like an artist beginning his first strokes of a new painting. Soon the November winds will bring the first snow. And the sound of leaves crunching under our feet will be replaced by the sound of the crisp winter's snow. Gone are the warm summer days of swimming at the lake. Long bike rides to the park. And yes, even the crack of a bat at a baseball game.

We now have our winter coats and gloves on to protect us from the winter's cold. Thoughts of hearty soups and homemade breads start to sound good on a cold November day. After a long hike in the woods with Jazz. Days are now becoming shorter and the air so crisp. And sometimes on a clear night, the stars are so bright. Just hanging out with that big old moon. Seems like you can almost touch them. Well, that's about it from my little town of Wellington. I better get going, I'm burning daylight and just about out of coffee.

Just sayin'.

One final thought. Take a second out of your busy day, say good morning to someone, hold a door open for them, watch their face light up and say thank you. And if they don't. You could kinda trip them going out the door. Just remember to wish them a nice day. Just sayin'.

Bruce and Jazz just Chillin

Photo was taken by Jan Hovater Middleton